What the critics are saying

2002 P.E.A.R.L. Best Erotic Nominee

Ms. Walder tells a wonderful tale that is at once intelligent and engaging. Once you enter this particular dream world, you may find yourself hoping that life IS but a dream .

- Amy L. Turpin, Timeless Tales

D0859127

Discover for yourself why readers can't get enough of the multiple award-winning publisher Ellora's Cave. Whether you prefer e-books or paperbacks, be sure to visit EC on the web at www.ellorascave.com for an erotic reading experience that will leave you breathless.

www.ellorascave.com

Ellora's Cave Publishing, Inc.
PO Box 787
Hudson, OH 44236-0787

ISBN # 1-84360-561-9

Edited by Martha Punches.
Cover art by Darrell King.

Warning: The following material contains strong sexual content meant for mature readers. *DREAM LOVER* has been rated HARD R erotic, by a minimum of three independent reviewers. We strongly suggest storing this book in a place where young readers not meant to view it are unlikely to happen upon it. That said, enjoy…

DREAM LOVER

Written by

CASSIE WALDER

Prologue

Edwina heard footsteps, heavy, masculine footsteps, coming down the hall towards the lab. Everyone who worked with her in the lab had long since gone home for the day.

"Liebling, have you not worked enough for one day?" Klaus asked impatiently in rapid German from the doorway.

She pressed the button on the remote control to turn off the security cameras. The security guards didn't need to see this reunion. Then she turned and smiled at him as she looked at the face she knew so well and loved. He was still wearing his heavy cashmere coat. Flakes of snow had not yet melted from the shoulders. The coat was unbuttoned revealing beneath it one of the dark worsted wool suits that he wore for business in the winter. He was every inch the successful businessman.

Still, she would have loved him even if he hadn't had two pennies to rub together. How could she not? He had swept her off her feet when they had first met and he had continually found new ways of making her fall more deeply in love with him. Sweet, strong, sexy – he was all that and more. She had loved him for years before she had met him.

She smiled at him. "Actually, I have a bit more work to do. Another couple of hours should be sufficient," she teased.

He shook his head negatively. "Nein, mein Frau. You work too hard and play too little. Come. The work will still be there in the morning. I am here now. Come play."

"Is that a request, or a command, Herr Baron?" she demanded softly as she unbuttoned her lab coat.

He walked towards her, lithe and graceful, like a panther stalking its prey. No man should be so beautiful, she thought. As he walked toward her, the expression on his face transformed into one of savage male hunger.

Her heart leapt. She felt her breasts tingle and begin to become hard. Her legs trembled. She felt herself grow wet in preparation for him. Her anticipation was so acute it was almost painful. She had expected him to be home today after an overseas trip. He had been away just over a month. The anticipation of reunion had been building all day.

"Do not push me Liebling," he warned lowly as he pushed her lab coat from her shoulders and down her arms. "I am at the edge of my control."

"Control is so over-rated Klaus my darling," she said lowly as she unfastened the single button that held the lined deep-green silk wrap dress together. She opened the dress to reveal her body, naked, except for the garter belt and stockings that he liked her to wear.

She watched him as he shuddered. Then she closed the remaining distance between them, wrapped her arms around his neck, and kissed him hungrily.

He backed her up against the wall. She reached down and unfastened his trousers and pushed them, and his boxers, out of the way. His penis was hot and heavy in her hand. How she wanted him!

A bottle of his favorite champagne was chilling waiting for them at home. There would be a light supper, soft lighting, softer music, and satin sheets on the big canopy bed. There would be time for gentle love play later tonight. But now was the time for quick, hot, and primal. She needed this as much as he did.

"Frau!" he moaned as she wrapped her left leg around his hip, under his coat, and guided him into her.

She had never felt more intensely female than she did at this moment. She felt every inch of his smooth, hard penis as he thrust hard into her, nudging her cervix. She cried out at his possession. This was her man, the only man she had ever loved, the only man she would ever love. The intensity of the love she saw on his face only made her love him more.

She had expected him to take her hard and fast. Yet he surprised her. He kissed her again, a kiss as gentle as any he had ever given her. His hands were softly tender on her breasts as he set about to give her as much pleasure as she gave him. She thought that she would die from the sensual torment of his hands on her breasts, her belly, her hips, and between her legs. When he licked his fingers then stroked them gently over her clitoris, she was certain of her impending death from pleasure. She was not about to tell him to hurry.

The control he was exerting showed on his face, in the cording of the muscles of his neck, and in the throbbing of his penis still deep within her. He allowed his control to slip only after the contractions of her climax began. Then, not letting her ease through that, he began the hard and fast possession that she had first expected.

Several moments later, she heard a cry and realized that it was hers. She was lost in the urgency of the moment. He held her tighter as his hips buckled one last time and hot semen spurted into her. Then he cried out.

A loud noise, not at all like a human voice, penetrated her consciousness. She was suddenly awake, alone, and in her bed in the apartment over the shop. The alarm clock was ringing loudly. It was five thirty and time to get moving. She reached over and hit the snooze button. Ten more minutes.

She had done it again. She had dreamed of him, dreamed of this man, Klaus, she had long loved and yet had never met. This was hardly the first time that she had dreamed of him with such intensity that the pleasure had breached the dream/reality barrier. The last throbs of her climax still lingered. She had long since ceased to be shocked by the intensity of the dreams.

Edwina groaned in protest as she sat up and swung her legs over the side of the bed. The shop needed one more hard day's work on it before it opened. Yet, before she did anything else, she needed to record this dream in her journal. She always journalized her dreams. Edwina reached for her eyeglasses and the current volume of her dream journal.

She wondered how many times she had dreamed of him over the years, how many times that they had made love together in her dreams. If she had been so inclined, she could have sat down with the volumes of her dream journal and counted the number of times that she had been with him in her dreams. She couldn't remember a night since her childhood that she hadn't dreamed of him. It was during her teenage years that the dreams had become profoundly sensual. The dreams probably numbered into the thousands. She had made love to him thousands of times, in a variety of positions, and the intensity had never been less than mind-blowing.

Quite a track record for a virgin, she thought with a ragged sigh.

No man she had ever met had ever even come close to tempting her to take him as a lover. After loving Klaus in her dreams for so many years, she judged every man by his standard. Every man she compared to Klaus came up seriously lacking.

No sooner than she had finished journalizing her dream, the temperature in the room dropped by a good ten degrees as the ethereal form of a young Victorian woman who called herself Catherine appeared beside her bed. Edwina's cats howled as they always did when Catherine popped in.

"Pleasant dreams?" the spirit asked dryly.

Edwina had almost, but not quite, gotten used to the experience of this spirit materializing. The paralyzing fear that she had felt the first few times that she had seen the spirit had numbed over the months into mere cautious disbelief. Edwina was still not comfortable with the presence of this ethereal personage, but at least now the presence didn't scare her completely witless or make her run to change her underwear.

"Go away, Catherine," Edwina said firmly. "I am entirely too busy this morning to listen to you."

"You are always too busy," the young woman sulked. "You're not letting me accomplish my assigned task. It is beyond merely annoying."

"You should have gotten the message by now. Go haunt someone else. You are not welcome here."

"That person of whom you dream is wrong for you, Edwina. Avoid him. For the sake of your immortal soul, avoid him."

"Go away, Catherine!"

The spirit winked out as suddenly as she had appeared, but there was a defiant expression on her face as she faded.

Edwina shook her head and went into the bathroom for a shower before beginning the work she had to do. It was going to be a very long day.

Chapter One

Klaus von Bruner stood just outside the door of the small garden shop that evening. It was a few minutes after seven. The sun had gone down some time before. The streetlights were on. On the glass door was painted in an elaborate Victorian-style font, "A Victorian Garden, Incorporated." Below that was written on the glass in a smaller sized font, "E.E. Johnson, Ph.D. CEO."

He tried the shop door and found it open. He walked in and stood there, his eyes fixed on her back as she stood on a library ladder arranging items on an upper shelf. Debussy's String Quartet Number 1 in G minor Op. 10 filled the air. It wasn't one of his favorite pieces but it was one that he could easily listen to with enjoyment. He didn't recognize the recording, however. It wasn't by any group that he recognized. Yet, the performance was quite polished. He wondered if this was some of her music.

For the moment, he was content just to look at her back as she worked. She wore a softly faded black denim skirt that fell in soft folds to mid calf along with a black silk turtleneck, black wool socks, and black leather running shoes. Her long red hair was pulled back neatly into a ponytail at the nape of her neck, fastened with a black cross-grain ribbon bow. The dark clothing only called more attention to her porcelain skin, tall and athletic frame, and flame colored hair. Even dressed casually, Edwina Johnson was one of the most exquisitely lovely women he had ever seen. She was a woman as beautiful inside as she was outside.

Edwina knew that someone had come into the shop. She had felt the temperature lower somewhat a few moments before. Was the presence she felt behind her human or spectral? Having encountered one of the spirits said to haunt the building, she was in no hurry to meet any of the rest of them about which Jim, one of her tenants, loudly complained. She could have sworn that she had locked the door behind her when she had come back in several hours before after running errands.

She knew that she had pulled the shades on the windows. She hadn't heard the buzzer on the door ring. She made a mental note to check that the door buzzer was working properly. She slowly came down the ladder. Only when she was firmly on the floor once more did she turn around to see who was in the shop.

Klaus? Klaus, here? Edwina had thought that she had only imagined him, conjured him out of her vivid imagination. Yet here he was. Or was he? She removed her eyeglasses with her left hand and rubbed her eyes with her right. Then she replaced her glasses on her face. He was still here. His presence wasn't a trick of her tired eyes.

She assessed him for a long moment. He was handsome, forty-something—raven haired with just a hint of gray at his temples—and dressed in the stark black and white of formal evening wear. He was clearly on his way to an event that called for dress wear. There were some men who were clearly uncomfortable in formal clothing. This man wore his evening clothes as though they were his second skin. She rather liked that level of confidence in a man. She liked the looks of him. *Period.*

He was not at all flashy. Yet, he definitely seemed solid, slim, with the build of a runner who also worked on his upper body. There didn't seem to be an ounce of spare flesh on him. In her dreams, she had touched his firm and muscular body many times. She knew his body as well as she knew her own. Or at least, she did in her dreams. Reality was another matter entirely.

She didn't need to look long at his face to realize that her dreams had been spot on. His eyes were gray/green. His facial features were not especially notable in and of themselves, but they went together in a very pleasing way. He was on the pale side. But he wore airs both of power and of bold virility with the same ease he wore his tuxedo.

"*Guten Abend*, Klaus!" she greeted him in rapid German as she crossed the room and extended her hands to him in greeting. Now, Edwina wondered, what made her treat him as though he were an old and dear friend? What possessed her to call him by name? She had to be utterly insane. What was she doing acting on her dreams? What if that was not his name? Had she made a fool of herself?

He seemed taken aback at the warmth of her greeting for a moment, and then he smiled at her, broadly, before he took her hand in his.

This man was solid and real, not a spectral entity, not a dream, not a mirage. Edwina didn't know if she was pleased with that or not. It always spooked her terribly for anything from her dreams to come true. This man was such a large part of a vast number of her dreams.

The way that he was looking at her made her feel more than a bit faint. Just being this close to him was arousing. She was astonished at how her body was reacting to this man. Her breasts were tingling. Her body instinctively began to prepare itself for mating. If this innocent contact was making her tremble, she didn't know how much more of his touch she could endure. The prospect of discovering how it would make her feel was exciting, almost too exciting.

"*Guten Abend*, Edwina," he said warmly.

He hadn't missed the widening of her eyes as he had taken her hand. He hadn't missed the tightening of her breasts. She obviously wasn't wearing a bra since her nipples were strongly profiled against the soft silk knit of her sweater. Those reactions were all the encouragement he needed. She was as drawn to him as he was to her. That was good. He could use that. At this point, he'd use whatever of her weaknesses he discovered. He had waited entirely too long for her. He hadn't anticipated her knowing who he was. However, he took that as encouragement.

Being this close to her, touching her and knowing that she was responding to him, was evaporating much of his remaining caution. All he could think about was how much he wanted her and how long he had waited for her.

He still held her hand in his. He raised her hand to his lips. Then, he gently turned her hand over. Lightly, tenderly, he kissed the back of her wrist as he watched her reaction. He could see the pulse in her wrist beat madly. Pure satisfaction coursed through him as he saw her response to his simple act. Her moist lips parted slightly, in invitation, and he doubted that she was aware of the small sound of yearning that had escaped her. He, on the other hand, was very aware of it. The sound burned a path to his groin. It was all he could do not to pull her into his arms. All he could think about was how good things were going to be between them. She was trembling at that lightest of caresses. How would she react to more?

Edwina found herself trembling. That light of a caress should not have sent her into such a tailspin. Yet it had. She pulled her hand away from him and stepped back. Maybe if she put a little distance between them, he wouldn't notice how she was trembling at his touch.

"I fail to recognize the recording of Debussy. Who are the musicians?" he asked after she stepped back from him.

The warmth of her face was a telltale sign that she was blushing. Of all her least favorite things about herself, her ability to blush was on the bottom of the list. But then again, most people with her fair coloring and red hair had that tendency. "That's merely a performance by three of my cousins and me," she answered, in English, as she reached into her skirt pocket and clicked the remote control on the CD player.

"It is an excellent performance," he said obviously impressed. "There is no need to stop the playing of the piece."

She shrugged. "Oh, it's passable for a group of amateurs. I was just reviewing the recording before we give it to our grandmother for her birthday Monday. And I can't listen critically to it and talk to you at the same time."

"The recording is a most unusual gift."

"It's a birthday gift for the woman who has everything," Edwina allowed. "It is one of her favorite pieces. Several of us were at a loss at what to get her for her birthday. This seemed to be a perfect solution. At least, we are reasonably certain that this recording will be a unique gift."

"You tend to think outside of the box, do you not?"

"I do try not to limit myself to conventional ways of approaching problems," she answered quietly.

He looked at her for a long time without saying anything. His frank assessment of her made her uneasy. Then he remarked, "It is a most unusual line of wares you stock."

The pithy comment that she was not among the wares stocked in the shop was on the tip of her tongue, but she bit that back. Instead, she said very politely, "Thank you. I try to meet the needs of both serious and amateur gardeners, as well as those who haven't the time or the inclination to do the work themselves but wish to have the benefits of a well-tended garden or the products of a garden. How may I serve you this evening?"

She was proud of herself that she had kept her infamous temper under control. Her anger at the moment was directed at herself for getting carried away by the flood of memories of dreams. Dreams weren't reliable. For all she knew, this man had a wife and six children at home. Just because she had fallen in love with the image of him in her dreams didn't mean either that he would reciprocate those emotions or that she would actually love him in reality.

He smiled.

That smile quite literally took her breath away. The glint in his eye told her without a doubt that this man was well-used to the effect he had on women. She couldn't help herself. She smiled back at him and waited for him to answer her.

"Have I irritated you in my frank appreciation of your beauty?" he asked softly, still speaking German. "I am afraid that I was rather rude. I do apologize for causing you embarrassment. That was not my goal, I assure you."

"And what is your goal, *mein Herr*?" she demanded in rapid German.

He gave her another of those breathtaking smiles. "No Field Marshal divulges his campaign plans to his opponent, *Fraulein*," he answered smoothly in his native tongue.

"Battle plans!" Edwina spluttered in English. "In what way are we at war?"

His smile became even broader as he answered her in English, "In the same elemental way that man and woman have always been at war, until they mutually conquer and surrender one to the other. I do not believe that the initial surrender will be long coming for either with us. You tremble at my touch and that quivering is not from fear. We desire one another greatly."

Edwina felt her face grow warm again. "Are you always so blunt?"

"Actually, I am usually far more blunt than I have been tonight," he replied with no apology, only self-knowledge, in his voice. "I have little patience for people who are less than straightforward. But that is a personal idiosyncrasy."

"I see," she replied not wanting to be drawn further into his banter in any language. She did not have either the time or the energy to become involved with him or anyone else right now. There was work to be done. Still, she knew from her dreams that he was a man who would demand nothing less than a woman's full devotion. However, the rewards for that devotion would be extraordinary. He would return many times over all the devotion lavished upon him.

"Do you see?" he demanded. "Perhaps you do at that."

"Since you have a great appreciation for bluntness, I'll ask these two questions. Why have you come?" Edwina demanded. "What do you want from me?"

"What do I want from you? Let's start with the simplest of things."

"By all means."

"Do you carry pennyroyal?"

Of all the things he could have asked for this was the most unexpected. She felt a surge of disappointment. Then she was upset with herself for feeling disappointed. He'd come into her shop. It was unreasonable to expect that he might want something other than some of the merchandise she stocked.

"To what use were you planning to put pennyroyal?"

"Why would you want to know that?" he asked softly, yet there was an edge of annoyance in his voice. This was clearly not a man who was used to being questioned about anything.

She looked at him over the top of her eyeglasses. It was a look that had been well known to make Freshman Biology students quiver in their boots back in her days as a doctoral candidate teaching assistant. But all he did was grin as though he was borderline amused at her mild effort to put him in his place.

"I should have thought that was obvious. The use determines the form of the herb you will need," she explained with exaggerated patience.

He thought about that for a moment before he replied, "Of course. The herb is for my dog, Brutus. I place loose pennyroyal in his bedding and put a few drops of essential oil on his brush when I groom him. A few drops of oil are all that is necessary. Yet my supply is nearly depleted of both oil and herb."

"Pennyroyal is far more pleasant smelling, and far less toxic, than most commercial flea remedies, at least for all male households," she told him easily as she moved to the mirrored display area where she kept the essential oils. She had thought he was right behind her, but the only reflection she saw in the mirror was her own face.

"How big is Brutus?" she asked as she turned around and gently placed the vial of essential oil upon the antique gray marble counter.

She saw with some relief that his attention was fixed on a set of bronze patio furniture near the back of the shop. He hadn't been behind her. Naturally, since he hadn't been there, there had been no reflection of him in the mirror. She mentally chided herself for having an overly active imagination.

It was a beautiful set of furniture at which he was looking. She wouldn't have taken it in on consignment if it had been other than beautiful.

She spoke, "Jeff, the man who made that set, holds a Masters of Fine Arts in Sculpture and does what he calls 'practical and original art for gardens'. If you like his style, but not that particular set, he will do commissioned work."

He turned to face the shopkeeper. "It is not a production run item, then?"

"No. All of his work is unique. He made that set on speculation for display in the shop. He never does two sets that are quite the same. He has a low tolerance for boredom. But much of that comes from the fact that he is utterly brilliant."

"I can believe that. The workmanship in the piece is absolutely extraordinary. It's quite beautifully made as well as being a handsome set of furniture."

"He's quite meticulous about his workmanship. Some artists aren't. But Jeff comes from a furniture making family. Granted, he doesn't make furniture like his father and grandfather did or that his brothers do. But, he's holding up the family tradition in his own special way."

He looked at the price tag once more. "You know him quite well then this artist Jeff?" he asked carefully.

Edwina wanted to tell him that this was none of his business. Instead, she explained, "Jeff keeps company with my cousin Emily. I suspect that they will marry someday. Neither of them however seems in any tearing hurry about taking that step."

The man smiled in what she thought was relief as he looked at her. "I see."

"Now, about your dog? What breed is he?"

"Brutus is a bull mastiff."

"A guard dog?"

"He is."

She'd bagged up dried pennyroyal earlier in the day to sell for dog bedding. She reached under the counter for a "large dog" bag of the herb. That went on the counter as well.

He walked over to the counter. "Why the qualification about this herb being suitable in an all male household?" he asked, obviously curious.

"Pennyroyal oil is a natural abortifacient. Taken internally, it can easily be lethal as it may cause massive hemorrhaging. If absorbed through a pregnant woman's skin it can lead to miscarriage. It may also birth defects in her unborn child, if it happens to prove non lethal to both mother and child."

"And yet you stock the herb."

"I am not a married woman," she replied quietly.

"Is that a guarantee that you will not become with child?" he asked quietly, a tone of disbelief, even world-weary skepticism, in his voice.

Edwina fought back her blush and lost. This conversation was entirely too embarrassing. "You ask many questions that are entirely none of your business."

"On the contrary, you are as drawn to me as I am to you. That makes everything about you my business, just as it makes everything about me your business. We will know one another as intimately as any man and woman ever can know one another. We will know each other better than most couples ever know one another."

Edwina might be able to deny the attraction she felt for him. She had never been a liar and wasn't about to begin now. She felt her face grow even warmer and knew that she was quite likely a bright shade of crimson. "You are presumptive, Klaus!"

"It is rare to find a beautiful woman who can still blush so beautifully," he said quietly as he came around the counter to her. "You are an incredible woman, Edwina

Elizabeth. However, I am not presuming anything. And you are quite enough of a woman to know that."

There was nothing at the moment that she wanted any more than she wanted to be in his arms. That strong desire, almost compulsion, to get close to a man whom she did not know except from her dreams shocked her. She had never thought of herself as a particularly wanton woman. If anything, she was considered by most people to be incredibly straight-laced, bordering on totally asexual. Only she was privy to her dreams and fantasies.

She did not resist as he pulled her into his strong embrace. She couldn't think of any place that she wanted to be more than to be held by him at this moment.

Klaus kissed her deeply, possessively, as if he had every right to plunder her mouth. His mouth moved on hers with an expertise that totally overwhelmed her. He tasted warm, utterly masculine, and completely addictive. But then again, that was how he had always tasted in her dreams. Being in his arms felt like coming home. Yet, his kiss was so intoxicating that she knew that she would have fallen had he not been holding her so tightly against him.

He held her even more firmly with one arm while the other hand tangled in her hair, adjusting her head so that he had full possession of her mouth. She was warm and sweet and so responsive that all he could think about was how they would be in bed together. Explosive would be the only word for it. Visions of silk sheets and her naked body writhing in ecstasy beneath him danced through his mind.

No other woman had ever tasted quite like her. No one else had ever shown him the same mix of emotions in a single kiss. Edwina gave him no practiced seduction, no well thought-out plan to entice, no sense of premeditation at all. She simply gave him freely from the fire in her soul.

He wanted more. He wanted everything that she could give him. He knew that he could take her, right here, right now. She would yield.

Yet, he wanted more than to simply possess her for a brief time. He wanted her permanently, completely. He needed her to come to him out of her own free will—a free, informed, and conscious choice. Seducing her, bending her to his will, was something he knew he could easily do.

Klaus knew that she would quite rightly resent that. Then her resentment would build a wall between them. He couldn't afford that, especially not now.

His lips left hers and she made a small whimper of loss.

"You make me lose my head," he said thickly as he held her tightly.

She forced herself to smile. "Good. I'd hate to think I was the only one affected."

"I am not presuming anything, am I, Edwina?"

"No," she admitted quietly. "You aren't presuming anything, Klaus."

He kissed her neck just beneath her ear. So fragile, so delicate, so alive! Klaus could feel her pulse beating beneath his lips. His tongue quickly darted out as he licked her tender skin.

She shuddered.

Her heart was racing—he could feel that. There was more than excitement in the way her heart beat. "You are afraid," he stated as he pulled away from her a bit. "You are afraid of me, Edwina?"

In the small part of her mind free from desire, Edwina was very much aware that he was correct — she was afraid. The desire was not surprising. She had been in love with him, or at least in love with him as she had dreamed of him, for most of her life.

The two of them, at least in her dreams, had shared an active, varied, and ultimately satisfying sex life. Part of her had wanted desperately to know if kissing him, loving him, would be as good in the flesh as it was in her dreams. The kissing was every bit as she had experienced it in her dreams. She was reasonably certain that the rest of it would be as good.

The fear was totally unexpected. She didn't know what to make of it. Yet she couldn't deny the reality.

"Klaus, be quiet and kiss me again." Even she heard the quiet desperation in her voice.

She didn't have to ask him twice. This time the kiss was hard, fierce with need, demanding everything, promising the universe. This was the caress of a man who fully intends to take his woman to bed.

Wildness nearly overwhelmed her. All she wanted was the man in her arms. She wanted him more than she thought she could want anyone or anything.

Able to resist anything except temptation where this woman was concerned, he allowed his hands to move until they cupped her unbound breasts through the silk of her sweater. He felt her nipples grow even harder under the warmth of his palm. When he gently flicked his thumbs against her nipples through the knit of the cloth, she drew a deep shuddering breath. He wrapped one strong arm around her waist and held her tightly as the other hand continued to tease her breasts.

He stopped kissing her and looked at her face.

"Klaus!" she moaned his name as she looked at him. She saw control fighting with wildness on his face. But under it all was tenderness and—dare she believe her eyes—love?

His eyes searched her face. "*Liebling,*" he answered quietly as the hand that was on her waist moved lower to cup the firm muscles of her bottom and pull her close against the hard ridge of his penis.

Her moan of pleasure and the instinctive shimmy of her pelvis against him was enough to strain his control nearly past the breaking point.

She felt him shudder and knew that he was fighting for the control that meant so much to him. She knew, at least from her dreams, just how wild that loss of control could be. It frightened her and thrilled her at the same time. There was danger with him. She knew deep within her soul that he would never hurt her. Yet as long as he thought she was afraid of him, he'd be very controlled.

Her pleasure became so intense, she didn't know if she could bear it. And then suddenly, the tension released in a wave of pleasure. She gasped, stiffened, and arched against him.

Masculine pride and sexual hunger warred within him for dominance as he held her tightly and let her gentle down from her orgasm. He was surprised, pleasantly so, to find her so responsive to him. Klaus kissed her once more.

"Edwina, you are extraordinary," he whispered as his lips moved from her mouth to her ear.

"What I am is profoundly embarrassed," she admitted lowly.

Then he shifted position until he was looking her in the face. He challenged her softly as she stood in his arms. "Look me in the eye after that and tell me that you don't want me. If you send me away, I will go and never bother you again."

She bit her bottom lip nervously as she fought her embarrassment. "I profoundly distrust anything that blooms this quickly. But, please don't go away, Klaus."

"My love for you is eternal."

"You are a romantic."

"You bring it out in me," he said as he stroked her face. He loved the way that she reacted to him, turning her head into his hand, as her face reflected the simple pleasure of a touch. He wanted to touch her all over. He wanted to be inside her when she had the next orgasm. He wanted to feel her muscles tighten convulsively about his penis as she reached her orgasm again.

"I'm not afraid." Yet, she didn't know which of the two of them she was trying to convince. She knew that she was lying—something she never did—and she suspected that Klaus knew that as well. She was afraid, terribly afraid. Yet, she didn't know what frightened her more— her reaction to him, the fact that her dreams about him were coming true, or the pure male magnetism of the man.

"Well, that makes one of us," he said softly as he lifted her skirt. "You frighten me, woman."

She drew a shuddering breath as his hand closed over the thin silk of her panties. "You're awfully bold for a frightened man," she answered.

His hand left her breast and went beneath her skirt as well. He tugged off her panties, letting them fall to the floor around her ankles. Then he placed his hands on her waist, lifted her off the floor, swung her around and sat her down on the high barstool that sat near the counter.

"Appearances can be deceptive," he said as he pocketed her panties. And then he kissed her again deeply, before she could reply.

"You've made your point, Klaus," she said lowly at the end of that kiss as his hands went beneath her skirt once more. "I'm putty in your hands."

"Not putty, but a warm and responsive woman." His fingers lightly stroked her pubic hair. "So warm…"

Edwina looked up at him. "Klaus!" she moaned and reached for him.

"No. Touch me and I'll lose what little control I have left. Put your hands down and keep them there, or touch your own breasts and add to your pleasure. Just don't touch me, right now, please. This is for you. Sit back, relax, close your eyes, and enjoy this small amount of love play. Let me give you this pleasure, Edwina."

He slipped his middle finger into her vagina even as he lightly alternately rubbed and flicked at her clitoris with his thumb. He gently, rhythmically, fingered her vagina. She was tight, wet, and hot. The tightness surprised him.

All he could think was how much he wanted to drop his pants and replace his fingers with his penis. She'd be so tight and hot around him—he could barely stand the thought. Any lovers she had ever had would have been some time ago. The suspicion was growing in his mind that she had never had a lover at all. Taking her as he wanted to–hard, fast, and deep–was sure to hurt her. The last thing that he ever wanted to do was to hurt her.

He concentrated on giving her pleasure. Long experience had taught him all the ways to drive a woman into ecstasy. As her breathing changed and he saw that she was close to release, he varied his rhythm. Klaus smiled as she arched and groaned his name a few short minutes later.

With a boldness that she didn't know she could demonstrate, she unfastened his trousers. She closed her hand around his rigid penis through the fabric of his silk boxer shorts.

He moaned.

She quickly snatched back her hand as though she were burned. "I'm sorry. I didn't mean to hurt you."

Klaus looked at her in disbelief. It was clear that she was really upset at the thought that she had hurt him. Between that reaction and the tightness he had discovered, Klaus was forced into the irrefutable conclusion that Edwina was a virgin. The confirmation of his suspicion was sobering.

She rushed into words before he could speak. He heard the sincerity in her voice, and the misery. "I just thought I might show you some of the pleasure you gave to me. I didn't mean to hurt you."

"You didn't hurt me," he said quietly with a small smile as he tried not to laugh. She wouldn't appreciate his laughing at her. And she wouldn't understand how charming he found her innocence. He refastened his trousers. "But this has gone far enough, much further than it should have, tonight. I didn't come here planning to seduce you."

"What did you plan?"

He smiled again. "To talk business. But I see that things will never be able to be totally businesslike between us."

"Complaining?" she teased.

"Not in the least, *Liebling*." He kissed her forehead, then walked away from her, coming to stand just on the other side of the counter once more. "While this is not the time, Edwina, I'm putting you on notice. I will soon take you to bed and keep you there, for days, weeks, or even months."

"*Months?*" she echoed on a disbelieving whisper. She didn't trust her legs to hold her, if she would stand, so she spun around on the barstool. "Which is why you just put distance between us," she answered in a far sharper tone than she wanted to use as she reached under the counter and tossed him a small packet containing a pre-moistened towelette. She kept a few of those on hand for when she was repotting plants on the counter. She had never even imagined a situation like this. She knew from the warmth of her face that she was blushing even more boldly than she had been a few moments before.

He smiled at her once more as he opened the package and unfolded the small towel. Not even once did his eyes leave her face as he cleansed his hands and wadded up the towel before tossing it in the trash. "Oddly enough, it is. Are you willing, Edwina, to give yourself to me right here, on the floor of your shop? Or perhaps you would rather be standing, with your back against the wall? Would you give yourself to me like this, knowing anyone could walk in on us, as I walked in here a few moments ago? My control is stretched so tightly that I almost wouldn't care."

She almost didn't care either. A few moments ago, she wouldn't have resisted him in the least if he had backed her up against the wall or lowered her to the floor. She would have followed him anywhere he led her. That much was painfully obvious to her. Yet, now a small shred of sanity was creeping back into her mind.

"No," she answered him quietly as her face grew even warmer. "That would not have been my preference in any sane moment. Of course, sanity has precious little to do with the way that you make me feel when I'm in your arms."

"I can think of many more suitable settings for the first time that we come together. It will not be rushed or clandestine, Edwina. Neither of us will have any cause for regret afterwards. It is only a matter of time. There is no doubt as to the eventuality. When we make love, it will be the best thing that ever happened to either of us. You can count on that. Yet, we are mature adults. We can wait until we have both privacy and time enough to fully enjoy one another."

She blushed and wanted to deny his statement about the inevitability of their making love, but couldn't. "Who are you trying to convince? Me or yourself?" she demanded.

"Perhaps both of us. I know that putting distance between us when all I wanted — still want — is to make love to you, was one of the most difficult actions I've ever taken."

"What else do you need this evening?"

"You really don't want me to answer that. If I did, you'd be blushing again from head to toe," he said gently. "I'm going to enjoy teaching you to becoming shockproof, my dear. I believe I shall miss those blushes. They are so utterly charming."

"Look, let's just keep try to get back to a businesslike tone, okay?" she offered shortly.

"No, it's not okay. However, I can see that I am making you profoundly uncomfortable. So just answer my question. Does your being unmarried mean that you can safely handle that herb?"

She looked at him for the longest moment while she tried to formulate words to express her dismay with this conversation. When she spoke, it was with measured words. "I don't have time for this."

He looked at her for a long time. She forced herself to meet his gaze, even though the heat on her face told her that she was once more crimson. "Don't evade. Time is an illusion. It is simply an artificial construct. Answer the question. Is it safe for you to handle this herb?"

"Time is not an illusion. It's a dimension in the Physics of Relativity. None of us can live in the ever present now," she dismissed.

"On the contrary, none of us ever lives otherwise than in the current moment, regardless of how long we live. One cannot live in more than one moment at a time."

"So you don't plan at all?" she challenged.

"Of course I do. Businesses run on plans. Yet time is not real, Edwina. It's a construct used only to relate events to one another. Beyond that it has absolutely no significance."

"You are really quite the philosopher, aren't you?"

"And you are quite adept at evading questions you don't want to answer."

"I believe that's my right, especially when the questions coming from a virtual stranger are so impertinent!"

"We will be many things to one another, but being strangers isn't one of them. Now is it?"

"No. It isn't," she admitted quietly.

"Why do you resist this chemistry between us?"

Edwina shook her head negatively. More than anything else in the world, she wanted a future with this man. She bit her lip as she looked at him. "If you call what just happened between us resisting, then I'd say that we have to redefine some terms."

"Is there a special man in your life?"

"Only in my dreams," she said with a small smile.

"Are you planning to take the veil?"

She shook her head again negatively. "I thought about it until I was about ten years old. However, if I had possessed any real plans in that direction, I'd have been cloistered and life professed by now. But I wasn't cut out for a life of poverty, chastity and obedience," she dismissed. "Poverty doesn't appeal. I like having a sense of ownership of things. And I can't even imagine a time that I would be humble enough to meekly obey anyone."

He smiled in return. "You definitely weren't created for perpetual chastity. You are a beautiful and responsive woman."

"Could we please change the subject?" she asked uncomfortably.

"Do your pleasure preferences run to those of your own sex?"

"Not that I've ever noticed!"

"Then what is there to understand about your resistance to the strong chemistry between us?"

"Again, I didn't notice that I was particularly resisting. I would have followed you anywhere that you took me, and you know it. The fact we are not on the floor with my legs wrapped around you, both of us lost in a sexual fog of need and pleasure, is entirely due to your strength of will, not mine."

"Keep stoking the fires, woman, and you may yet get a good view of the ceiling this evening," he warned quietly in German. "My control is nearly exhausted."

"No. I'm now on guard against you. You won't blindside me twice," she answered him in English.

"Did I blindside you?" he asked lowly, in English. "You really categorize what happened between us as my taking advantage of you?"

"No. I'm shocked at my behavior. Yet you didn't take advantage. I should have stopped this at any one of several places, and I failed to do so. The fault is mine, not yours."

"I fail to see that there is any fault here at all. Which brings me back to my initial question. Is it safe for you to handle pennyroyal? You are not in a position to risk your life and the life of an innocent in handling this herb?"

"I don't stock anything that isn't safe for me to handle. I am in no hurry at all to meet Saint Peter. And death by exsanguination, which would be how one would die from pennyroyal poisoning, has never particularly appealed to me."

"Hmmm... I can think of much worse ways to die... But that is beside the point. Many people are not aware of the harmful or potentially harmful effects of herbs," Klaus said quietly, thoughtfully. "I am glad that you are at least aware of what you are doing."

"I am usually aware of exactly what I am doing at any given time," she said.

"Except when you are in my arms," Klaus added softly. "Then I make you mindless, don't I?"

"You don't need me to answer that question."

"Yes. I do. Edwina, please tell me that you were just in my arms because that was where you wanted to be?"

She couldn't contain the blush when she thought about just how much she had wanted, still wanted, to be in his arms. "The last man who tried to force his attentions on me ended up in an untidy heap on a boulevard in Paris— nursing a broken knee," she said harshly. "I am certainly capable of taking care of myself, Klaus."

He looked at her for a long moment. Then he smiled. "I believe I should like to hear that tale sometime."

"No. I don't think so. It's rather ordinary, actually. Now is there any merchandise that I can get for you tonight, besides the herbs?" she asked, pointedly changing the subject.

"You seem to know great deal about herbs."

She shrugged, grateful for the change in subject. "Herbs have always been a serious interest of mine. That's why I wrote a book on the subject. Medicinal herbs and herbs used in various cultural and religious rituals have always been a fascination to me."

"You fascinate me."

She sighed. "Then you have a low fascination factor, indeed," she said dryly.

He shook his head negatively. "No. People have to be quite interesting for me to take especial notice of them. You are the singularly most fascinating woman I've run across in some time."

She sighed and shook her head. "I fear, then, that you have lived an extremely sheltered life."

Edwina noted that his eyes momentarily grew hard at that comment. She realized that she had inadvertently given him offense. Not knowing what else to do, she said quietly, "I am sorry. I meant to give no offense."

The man nodded negatively. "None taken. When you intend to give offense, Doctor Johnson, you do so ruthlessly."

Edwina suspected that he was repaying her in kind, with his comment about ruthlessness, for her comment about his sheltered life. That his comment was accurate was hardly immaterial.

He continued, seriously, "As for your comment, it was merely the recognition of a truth. You are unusually perceptive. Not many people are truly all that perceptive."

"Is there anything else related to the shop with which I can help you this evening?" she said, changing the subject rapidly.

The last thing, besides her reaction to him, she wanted to discuss was perceptions, or what other needs he might have. They had already covered that subject of his needs in far more detail than she was comfortable discussing with strangers, even strangers that she felt she knew so intimately. Besides that, she preferred to deal in areas that she could both quantify and control. Her perceptions were not one of those areas.

He laughed, genuinely amused. "Kindly do me the honor of being my dinner companion tomorrow evening."

She noted that it wasn't a question, but rather a command. She was quite tempted to say yes. But she didn't. "No. Thank you."

Turning down his invitation was difficult for her. This man was entirely too tempting. Spending time alone with him would definitely not be a good idea just now. She was entirely too vulnerable where he was concerned. Surely the happenings of a few moments ago were adequate demonstration of that?

"You have other plans for tomorrow night?"

"I thought I'd give both my cats a bath."

His eyes twinkled with mischief. "That should be interesting," he allowed. "I'd almost pay to see that."

Edwina felt herself respond to his suppressed laughter with a genuine smile. "Almost? I'm deeply disappointed," she teased.

"I can tell. Now, what's the real reason you won't go out with me, Edwina?"

"You will quite likely think this is funny. Heaven knows that I'm finding it quite ironic at the moment, given the fact that we've already demonstrated that you have the definite ability to reduce me to a quivering lump of sensual jelly. The simple truth is that I do not date strange men. There are entirely too many untrustworthy people in the world, people who appear to be one thing and are actually another thing entirely," she said matter-of-factly. "Getting a proper introduction and reference is a small measure assuring a safeguard against all sorts of unpleasantries I'd rather not deal with. While we have rather skipped many steps in that process and rushed into a high degree of intimacy, I still don't know you."

She hadn't thought it was possible, but his smile became even warmer. "You are a decidedly old-fashioned female," he observed.

"If that were to be an actionable charge, I'd have to plead guilty," she replied easily. "I am extremely...conservative. Some would say that I'm an antique."

"You are definitely precious," he replied gently, with affection in his voice. "There aren't many mature women in this era who are virgins."

She felt her blush return in full force.

"You are a virgin, Edwina. Are you not?" Klaus demanded.

Again, she didn't see any reason to deny it. "Yes."

He looked at her questioningly. "You are a beautiful, passionate, woman. Why have you never taken a lover?"

"Perhaps I was waiting for a man I couldn't intimidate," she said quietly.

Klaus smiled. "I see."

Another man came into the shop before Klaus could reply further. The door buzzer did not ring. Edwina made a note to look at that. "*Herr* Baron, the Opera will begin soon," the man said in rapid German. "If you are to arrive before the curtain goes up, you must come soon."

"*Danke* Schmidt," Klaus replied, in the same language. "I shall be there in a few moments."

She smiled, then spoke to Klaus in rapid German "You will enjoy the production of *Don Giovanni*. I saw it in dress rehearsal the week before it opened in January. You will regret it profoundly if you are late. The herbs come to twenty dollars and seventy five cents."

"You like Opera?" he asked in German.

"I simply adore Mozart," she told him in the same language.

"Come with me, see it in full production," he offered, still in German. "Surely a dress rehearsal is not the same as a full production. And if you truly love Mozart, this is one Opera that you must experience with full production values. I have a spare ticket that will simply go to waste otherwise. I should very much like to see it used by someone."

"Date stand you up?" she teased, in English, although she couldn't imagine any female alive standing this man up for a date. Edwina knew that she the only way that she would break a date with this man was if there was a death in the family—her own.

He smiled again, but he spoke in English, "Not precisely. My sister, Karen, decided that she was going to spend her birthday with friends in Geneva. That sounded like more fun to her than spending it at the Opera with her stodgy older brother."

She shook her head negatively. "One day, she will regret that. Family is important. Friends come and friends go. But, family is a constant, or as much of a constant as anything is in life."

"True," he agreed quietly. "Yet, I believe that she is concentrating her interest on family, or at least on potential children, as represented by a young man whom she has been seeing. She was more interested in spending her birthday with him than with her stodgy middle-aged brother."

"Oh, cut that out! You are not 'stodgy'."

He smiled at her. "Then how would you describe me?"

Edwina shook her head negatively. "That's a loaded question."

"It certainly is," he agreed. "Are you going to answer it?"

"No, I don't believe I shall. You're going to be late to the Opera. Are the herbs all I can get for you this evening?"

"An affirmative answer to my offer would be quite welcome," he said.

"That's not going to happen. I cannot go with you to the Opera."

"You certainly are able to accept the spare ticket. Come and enjoy the Opera. There are no strings attached, *Fraulein* Doctor. I will be on my best behavior. You have my solemn word as a gentleman."

She couldn't help it. She laughed. His expression was so hopeful. Her first inclination was to say yes, leave the work, and go. This man was compelling. But she knew that she couldn't leave the work. There was just too much to do to take the time right now.

She sighed. "No. Sorry. I am hardly dressed for the Opera. And there is no time for me to change into suitable clothing, even if I was to be so inclined, without making you profoundly late for the performance."

"I can deal with being late."

Edwina smiled. "Just go and enjoy the production," she dismissed reluctantly. "I would no more go to the

Opera as the guest of someone whom I didn't know than I would have dinner with that person. That's final."

"Very well. You shall not be my guest. I will trade you this extra ticket for a year's supply of pennyroyal. The ticket is yours with no strings, bartered freely. Come and enjoy the music. You are under no obligation to me. You can even get your own transportation if that makes you feel better about it."

She smiled softly. The offer was tempting. But she couldn't take it. "No, thank you. I have seen the production. Besides, I really have too much to do here if I am to be absolutely ready for the opening of my shop tomorrow. Work does come before pleasure."

"When one is occupied with one's true life's work, work is pleasure."

"I would agree with that."

"Is this shop your life's true work?"

She smiled and shook her head negatively. "Let's just call it is a working vacation."

He removed his wallet from his inner coat pocket. He placed a hundred dollar bill on the counter. "Very well, if you are certain that you will not barter the ticket for the herbs, this should more than cover the cost."

"Oh dear. I'm not open for business officially yet. I have limited money in the till. I cannot change that."

"I fear that I have nothing smaller. Will you take a charge plate?"

She shook her head negatively. "My authorization to do so does not begin until tomorrow. So, please have the herbs as a gift," she offered, quite eager to have this disturbing man gone from the shop. "Or take enough of the herbs so that you have a large supply. Flea season will be upon us in earnest soon. You will need these things for your dog."

He smiled at her. "Do I make you nervous?" he asked.

"That's a stupid question. Of course you make me nervous. Only a fool wouldn't be nervous. And I've seldom — accurately — been called a fool."

He smiled. "You are truthful. Know this, Edwina. I will never harm you, or allow any harm to come to you. You are absolutely as safe with me as you want to be. Always."

"I have no doubt of that."

"I gently care for the people who are dear to me."

"I've been taking care of myself for a very long time. Here. Take back your money. Accept the pennyroyal as a gift."

"Take the money. Open an account for the excess. I am quite certain that we have not done our final business with one another. Lock the door after me. Anyone could have walked in on you." Then he gathered his things and was out the door before she could ask him his last name.

Quickly, securely, she triple locked the door behind him once he was outside. Then she lifted the edge of the window shade and looked out. She stood there and watched him climb into the back of his big black limousine. She watched the luxury car with the dark windows drive away.

Chills ran down her spine. The man knew her name. And she didn't know whom he was or where to find him.

She wasn't sure she liked having any part of her dreams about him confirmed. In fact, she was completely certain that she didn't like it. Nor, did she like the fact that she had let him leave without getting his full name. But one thing she was sure of, he had purposefully not introduced himself. It was part of some grandiose plan of his. She wasn't sure that she liked that either. After he was gone, she locked down the bars on the front window and door. Then she quickly went back to work.

The shop was slated to open in the morning. Yet the shop wasn't yet quite ready for the public. There was still quite a bit of work to be done. She didn't have time to think about that man. She could not get him out of her mind.

Who was he? Why had he come here, tonight of all nights? Had he simply seen the lights on and decided to stop on the odd chance that the shop would carry herbs? Nothing about that scenario seemed in keeping with the man's personality. He seemed to be far too organized and driven to be doing anything on the spur of the moment. He had planned this meeting.

"Yeah, right," she argued with herself. "So that invitation to the Opera was planned?"

The more she thought about the man, the more confused she became. She couldn't deny the fact that she found him both exciting and appealing. All Edwina knew, for certain, was the man utterly fascinated her. He had fascinated her for a very long time. Who was he, really? What did he want? Why did she find him so interesting?

She'd been around handsome and forceful men all her life. None of them had made her heart flutter the way this man did. None of them had made her want to abandon a lifetime's training in ethics as this man had. She had wanted, had felt nearly compelled, to leave everything and go with him. She had wanted to say 'yes' to his dinner invitation. She had wanted to spend the evening with him at the Opera. If truth were to be known, she wanted to spend more than just the evening with him. His idea of taking her to bed and keeping her there for days or weeks sounded awfully good to her.

Catherine's form materialized out of nothing in front of her in the shop. The ambient temperature in the room went down by exactly ten degrees. Edwina had forbidden the shade to enter her greenhouses for that reason. The plants could not tolerate the sudden temperature changes.

"As a matter of fact, that's one creature who doesn't do anything without planning it out well ahead of time," the shade said. "He has plans for you, my dear."

"What sort of plans?"

"I can't tell you more than that, except to warn you that seduction is the least of his designs for you."

"Why can't you say more than that?"

"It would be against the rules. I can't interfere in the ways of the living," the shade said. "I have already come perilously close to the line. I will not cross it."

"Convenient rules you have there, Catherine," Edwina replied.

"Not especially," the shade acknowledged wryly. "I can tell you this. You must be extremely careful around him. He wants to possess you — body, mind, and soul. And he'll use any method he has to use to get that job done. He's dangerous to you, Edwina."

"How so?"

The shade shook her head. "I have told you more than I should have. I can tell you nothing more."

"I've got work to do. Go away."

Catherine faded out.

Edwina shook her head negatively. "I've gone completely over the edge talking with a figment of my imagination."

The shade faded in again. Edwina felt the temperature drop once more. She turned around and faced the shade.

"I am not a figment of your imagination, Edwina. I am very real," the shade said.

"I'm not quite certain I believe that."

The apparition smiled softly. "I know that you are still uncertain. This is part and parcel of all that academic training of yours. You have been trained to question everything. Some things, Edwina, you must simply accept because they are."

"I don't question everything."

"Don't you?" Catherine demanded.

"Maybe I do. So tell me about the gentleman who was just here?"

The shade shuddered. "That one is no gentleman, believe me. He's ruthless going after what he wants. At this time, you are what he wants. Be careful. Be very careful around him. Don't trust him. He's dangerous. And that's all I'm going to say about him."

"Who is he?"

"That, my dear, is precisely the wrong question," the shade said as she faded.

Chapter Two

Edwina didn't have time to wonder what the right question would be. Very quickly, she returned to work finalizing stocking and making sure that everything would be ready for the opening.

She could not quite get him off her mind. She had known him intimately in her dreams for so many years that she could not help comparing her dreams to the reality of his existence. There was one thing that she knew without a shadow of a doubt. She found him fascinating. Make that two things—he wasn't going to disappear. He wanted something from her, something important to him. Now that he had made his presence known to her, she would be seeing him often. There was no doubt of that.

Edwina wasn't at all sure how she felt about any of this. On one hand, she was excited. On the other hand, she was afraid. Overall, she was suspicious.

He'd called her beautiful. She was under no illusions that she was beautiful, not at least in any classical sense of that word. Several of her cousins were classically beautiful. Yet Edwina had always been and still was too tall, too freckled, and too angular in her figure to be considered particularly beautiful.

Oh she wasn't ugly. Small children never had run screaming from her. While her female cousins and friends had boyfriends, Edwina had always had boys who were friends. When she had been beyond the stage of keeping company with boys, she had men friends. Very few of those men over the years had expressed a desire for the friendship to progress into something more intimate.

She had always been comparing those friends to the lover she had always embraced in her dreams. Compared to the man of her dreams, her male friends had faded into insignificance. She realized that whether she had wanted to do so or not, she had spent most of her life waiting for this man to make himself known to her.

Now Klaus, her dream lover, had appeared unexpectedly on her doorstep. What she was going to do about him was another matter entirely. He had called her beautiful. Every woman was entitled to the fantasy that a fine man thought her beautiful.

Was he a fine man? That was the question. If he were pouring on the charm in order to achieve another goal, to wrest some advantage from the relationship, then clearly he was not a fine man. There was something very strange about this meeting—something that she didn't care for at all. Yet she couldn't quite define it, other than her unease at having her dream lover suddenly appear.

Edwina gave the shop one final look-over at midnight before she shut off the lights and went upstairs to her apartment. She had bought this building simply because she could put the shop downstairs in the one empty street level shop space and easily live upstairs above the shops, having plenty of room for her experimental greenhouse.

Heather the cat walked up to her and rubbed herself against Edwina's leg. Picking up the sleek Siamese cat, Edwina walked over to the window seat in the front window of her upstairs apartment and sat down.

The phone rang. She answered the phone by reciting the number.

"Edwina Johnson?" Klaus asked. His voice was unmistakable as she had heard it often enough in her dreams.

"Who wants to know?"

He laughed, then spoke in rapid German, "*Fraulein*, I wish that you would consent to having dinner with me at a restaurant of your choice this evening."

"To whom am I speaking?" Edwina demanded, answering him in equally rapid German.

He laughed again. "My name is Klaus von Bruner. You sold me some pennyroyal a few hours ago. Do you recall?"

A shiver ran down her spine. She hadn't ever heard his last name, in spite of the years of the dreams. Von Bruner. That name sounded vaguely familiar. There was a family connection to some von Bruner family of Bavaria. But how they were connected was vague in her mind. She'd have to ask her grandmother for more details on that. She had only been half listening all those times that her grandmother had seemingly endlessly lectured her on the family history.

"My memory is unimpaired, *Herr* von Bruner," Edwina said quietly.

"*Don Giovanni* was excellent. You would have enjoyed it greatly."

"Indeed, I expected nothing less from the performance, since the dress rehearsal was so very good. I am glad that you enjoyed the Opera."

"I would have enjoyed it more with you beside me."

"No, I don't think so. I think we would have been all too absorbed with one another to even hear the music. At least this way, one of us had the chance to enjoy it. That's better than both of us being there, and neither of us enjoying the music because our minds were absorbed with fantasies about the other."

She could hear the masculine satisfaction in his voice, as he answered, "You may be correct in that, *Liebling*. You may well be correct. Do you fantasize about me?"

Edwina wondered why was she being so up-front with him. Was it because he had stated a preference for straightforwardness? Or was it because she—deep down—trusted him, as she had never trusted anyone else? She didn't want to think about this too deeply.

"Edwina? Are you still there?"

"Yes."

"Have dinner with me after your shop closes today?"

"I have given you my answer once, Herr von Bruner. It remains a resolute no."

"Dare I ask why you hesitate?"

"I am certain that you would dare to ask any question that crosses your mind. I have not seen any lack of boldness in your manner. If anything, perhaps you could use instruction in not speaking your mind quite so bluntly."

He laughed in genuine amusement. "I am a blunt man."

"I had noticed."

"Would you kindly explain yourself as to why you will not dine with me?"

"I am under no obligation to give you any answers. I've already told you why I had turned down your earlier invitation. You are a stranger. I do not know you. I do not know people who have told me that they know you. I do not socialize with strangers. It's just that simple."

"You don't socialize with strangers, but you would have gone anywhere this stranger led you," he stated smoothly. "Had I not backed away, you would have given your virginity to me without reservation, would you not have?"

"My behavior was an aberration. I'm not particularly proud of it."

"No, my dearest, it was not an aberration," he said sharply. "Were I with you right now, you would respond exactly the same way to me, and you know it."

"I assure you that I have never displayed that degree of wantonness before in my life!"

He offered softly, "That should tell you something rather important about the attraction between us, Edwina. Should it not?"

"It tells me that being alone with you is not a safe action to take at the moment, and may never be a safe action. And that I should probably avoid it at all costs."

"You are as safe with me as you want to be, Edwina. I will never take anything from you that you do not freely give."

"That, *Herr* von Bruner is the problem," she replied. "You touch me and I forget about a lifetime of habits of caution. I don't know you. I don't know anything really about you. Where do you come from? What do you value? How do you spend your time, aside from seducing women and attending operas? We're clearly compatible physically. There's no denying that. I wouldn't even try to. Still, sex, love, and commitment are inviolably tied together in my mind. I don't know enough about you to commit. Yet you own my body. It's all very confusing."

"I know it is confusing for you. My body, my soul, are yours as well, Edwina. I am your devoted servant."

"Are you?"

"Of course I am. I will give you anything that you want. What do you want?"

"A proper introduction and reference would be a beginning."

"You are an old-fashioned lady," he observed. "It seems I shall simply have to secure an introduction and references from one of your close personal acquaintances. Then you would no longer have an excuse—I would be known, to you and yours. I am certain it would be no difficulty to secure an introduction. We do have mutual friends."

"Who?"

"You might be quite surprised."

"That would still be no guarantee I would socialize with you," she warned dryly, in German. "I know a great many men with whom I will not date. And frankly, you frighten me."

"Now, Edwina, you said earlier that you weren't frightened of me."

"Upon further reflection, I've changed my mind."

"Ah, *Liebling*, are you frightened of me, or of your reaction to me?"

"I don't know, Klaus. I just don't know. I've been trying to decide that myself."

"Fair enough, Edwina. We have given each other much to think about this night."

"Above everything else, you are a fair man," she added in English.

"I always try to be so. Very well," he said, not at all perturbed by her switch of languages or by her answer, "I stand suitably warned. By the way, did you think of me?"

"What do you believe?"

"I believe I have been very much on your mind, my dear."

"That's what you wanted, isn't it?"

"Only the very beginning of the desire," Klaus answered. "Shall I tell you what else I desire?"

"I'd be most interested in knowing what you really want from me," Edwina said firmly. "I'm not exactly a woman who inspires any large degree of passion in men. So what do you really want from me and why are you trying to manipulate me with sex in order to get it?"

He was quiet for a long moment. "That is blunt speaking indeed. And it is incredibly wrong. Who made you doubt your beauty or desirability, Edwina?"

"I do want an answer to my question. What do you really want from me? Besides sex?"

"I will leave you to make up your own mind as to what forces compel me to seek you as we grow to know one another. Yet, know this—I am determined to win your heart."

"There are those who would say that I have no heart to win, or if I do that my heart—like a winter road—is ice covered and hazardous."

"You are purposefully attempting to discourage me. Why?"

"Why don't I let you figure that one out? I'm sure that I'm not the only one who is a habitual analyzer of events and people."

He laughed. She wished that she didn't love the sound of his laughter so. "Very well, Edwina. I shall think about it."

"It is late, or rather quite early," she replied in German.

"It is."

"Why are you calling me now?"

"You were on my mind, Edwina."

"You are aware, of course, that this is an incredibly inconvenient hour at which to call anyone."

"You were up. I suspect you have not been long out of your shop after putting the last minute before opening touches on it."

"You suspect? Or are you having me watched?"

"You are suspicious, aren't you?"

"Just answer the question. Are you having me watched?"

"I've not hired surveillance."

There was something about the way he said that. Edwina couldn't quite put her finger on it, but it made her profoundly suspicious.

"Who is paying for the surveillance, then?" Edwina demanded. "And how did you get the report in real time?"

Klaus was quiet for a long moment. "Are you always this suspicious?"

"Not always," she admitted.

"Then I make you uneasy?"

"Don't flatter yourself."

"I fear that I must. You do not seem willing to do so."

Edwina couldn't help it, a giggle bubbled up from within her. This man made her happy just talking to him. "Is your ego so fragile that it needs constant attention?"

"There are some who would say it needs constant feeding and stroking otherwise its' owner runs the risk of becoming an ogre."

"You have a decidedly warped sense of humor, von Bruner."

"So I have been told. Not always by persons who were quite as amused by my sense of humor as you appear to be."

"That, *Mein Herr*, I can well believe."

"Rest well. We shall meet again soon, Edwina. And I shall hold you in my arms then and make you know just how I cherish you."

"Somehow, I do not doubt that we shall meet again in the least. Good night."

"Are you that eager to bring this conversation to an end?"

"Not particularly. I should be, but I'm not."

He laughed quietly. "I know an all night coffee shop within walking distance of your apartment. Care to come out for a cup of coffee with me?"

"No, thank you."

"What could a cup of coffee hurt?"

"Probably nothing," she admitted quietly. "Other than keep me awake when I need to sleep tonight."

"They have decaffeinated and herbal teas."

"No, thank you. Going to a coffee shop will eat into my sleep time."

He laughed. "I shouldn't care to deprive you of your beauty sleep."

She couldn't help but smile as she teased him. "Why? Am I in eminent danger of becoming a hag?"

"On the contrary, you are so beautiful that it makes my arms ache to hold you. If you won't come out for coffee, how about going for a walk? The air is just brisk enough to give me an excuse to hold you tightly as we walk."

"You hardly strike me as a man who needs excuses to do anything that he wants to do. I think of you as the type who knows what he wants and goes to whatever lengths he has to in order to acquire the desired object."

"As I said before, you are unusually perceptive."

"What do you want from me?" she asked again.

"You do not ask easy questions. Where shall I begin?"

"At the beginning."

"I'll be outside the door of your shop in twenty minutes. We can talk in your apartment."

"Not a chance. First, if I don't know you well enough to have dinner with you in a fairly public restaurant, I definitely don't know you well enough to invite you into the privacy of my home. Second, it is far too late for me to be entertaining anyone. I'm tired and need to get to sleep soon. And third, most important of the bunch, I don't trust myself alone with you."

"Because you want me as much as I want you."

"There is no sense in denying the obvious."

"Edwina, invite me up."

"*No!* Absolutely not."

"I'm not a patient man, Edwina," he warned.

"Tough. I'm not particularly impetuous, Klaus."

"Then we shall balance out the faults in the other's character quite well."

Edwina smiled. She wished that she could believe that. "What do you want from me?" she demanded again.

"Right now, I can think of nothing I would want more than to have you in my arms, to kiss you, and to carry you to bed. I want to look at your face as you come apart in pleasure while in my arms. I want to hear the little sounds of desire come from your throat as we make love to one another. I want to lie in your arms and listen to you breathing as you fall into the exhausted sleep of a woman well and truly loved. And when you awake, I want to make love to you again."

"Is sex all you want from me?" she asked quietly, trying not to let her disappointment color her voice. "A man like you could get sex anywhere he wanted it. I'm sure you could telephone any number of women who would gleefully come running at your request. So, why come to me? These aren't games I play."

"Sex only a beginning, *Liebling*. Eventually, you will come to love me. Until then, I can make do with the passion I find in you. Through the heat of passion and frequent possession you will come to love me."

She wasn't going to tell him that she already loved him. That would be giving him entirely too much ammunition. "What else do you want?"

"I want to watch you as your belly blooms with new life. I want to be with you as you give birth to our children. I want to watch you nurse our babies. I want to be with you as you comfort our children as they grow. I want to sit beside you in church as our children marry. I want to hold our grandchildren, and see your features on their faces."

"That's a substantial list of wants," Edwina replied quietly. The mental pictures that he painted were profoundly appealing. But she knew that time was working against her. "I'm thirty-five, Klaus. Babies are considerably less of a possibility than they would have been ten years ago."

"Everyone has a list of wants, Edwina, a list of dreams wanted for one's life. What do you want? What would make you the happiest?"

"What do I want? Nothing other than what everyone wants deep down, I suppose. To be loved and accepted for who I am."

"And who are you, Edwina Elizabeth Johnson?"

"Who do you think that I am, Klaus Matthias von Bruner?"

Now, where did that middle name come from? Edwina wondered.

He was quiet for a moment. "Ah, you have been curious about me, then?"

"What can I say, you are a curious man."

"Yes. I am. But, I will grow on you."

"Like lichen on a rock?" she teased.

"More like understanding in a mind, expanding knowledge until it meets and perhaps exceeds natural ability."

Edwina was silent for a long moment.

"Are you still there, *Liebling*?"

"Do you always make up your mind so rapidly upon meeting a person?"

"No."

"Then why are you pushing me this quickly?"

"You are entirely too strong a person for anyone to push around. If I am to influence you to come along with me, in any respect, it will be because that is what you want to do, Edwina. We both are all too aware of that fact."

"I'm very tired now, Klaus. Goodnight."

"Sleep well, *Liebling*. God give you gentle dreams."

She returned the phone to the charging cradle after he disconnected. The man wasn't going to take 'no' for an answer. She rather liked that. And it frightened her more than a little bit, especially coupled with the long history of having dreamed of him.

"Whatever else Klaus von Bruner is, kitty," she said to Heather, "He is obviously resourceful. My private phone number is unlisted."

Heather, ever wise, simply replied with a "*Meyouw*."

"You know, Heather Cat, I bet that I could find out who this man is," she said mostly to herself.

Again, Heather said only, "*Meyouw*."

Edwina put down the cat and crossed over to her den, a room that did triple duty as her library, computer room, and guest bedroom. It was a large room she used all the time, and one that she had "wasted" a lot of money on. A vented gas fireplace with a white stone façade was a feature of the room. It was flanked by bookcases. Her computer desk sat in the corner nearest the door. A conversation grouping of furniture, including a sleeper sofa, sat cozily before the fireplace. Over the fireplace, she had hung a large framed canvass she had bought from a street artist in Paris. The scene was of a park. Children were playing. It wasn't a work of exceptional artistic merit, but it was full of joy and that was reason enough to hang it. The painting made her feel happy just to look at it.

She powered up the computer and connected to the Internet. She did a search for him. What she found was quite interesting. He was the CEO of a multi-national pharmaceutical products company. He held both a M.D. and a Ph.D. in biochemistry. He sat on several boards of charities funding research for genetic disorders.

She had interviewed with his corporation after she had finished her second doctorate. When the recruiter would not promise her in writing that she could pursue her own interests in research, she had walked away from the interview, giving them a polite "thanks, but no thanks" as an answer to their quite amazingly generous contract offer.

Catherine faded in. "He's been keeping track of you since he read your first dissertation, Edwina. You fascinate him. He thinks you have answers for him."

"What kind of answers?"

"He desperately wants you to work on a health problem that he has. And he'll do anything in his power to get you to do that, and I mean anything. He's not a creature to underestimate. He's both wealthy and powerful. Powerful in ways that you can't even begin to imagine. He could hurt you terribly, Edwina. Be careful."

"What problem could he have that he would need me to work on? He has an entire staff of people working for him who are just as qualified as I am, if not more qualified."

"You wouldn't believe me if I told you. Just be careful, Edwina. You are a nice woman. I don't want to see you hurt by him," the shade said.

"Right now," Edwina said. "I'm going to bed. Sunrise will be here before I know it."

"Don't forget to say your prayers," the shade replied in a tone of warning. "If you are going to deal with that creature, you'll need all the help you can get. I cannot interfere in this. I've broken so many rules as it is by warning you about him." Then she faded away.

Edwina went to her bathroom. As she undressed for her shower, she felt her face grow warm as she remembered how he had taken her panties from her. She took a long hot shower before she headed off to bed.

She awoke screaming from a nightmare a few hours later. Klaus von Bruner was in the lead of a pack chasing her through the night. There was something malevolent about him, and about all the others who were chasing her, something sinister, dark, unholy, inhuman. She was left with impressions of fangs and giant bats.

That was simply crazy. She had never dreamed of him as malevolent before. This dream wasn't of the same detail or feeling as her other dreams about him. This dream was shadowy, uncertain, and surrealistic.

Thinking of it, she couldn't grasp the dream in concrete detail. It was not at all like her normal dreams. She always remembered the details of her dreams.

All she really knew was the dream had frightened her, terribly.

Edwina switched on the light.

As she did, she noticed that Catherine faded in and the room grew cold. "It's not just in your dreams. Von Bruner's dangerous. His kind are dangerous," the shade warned. "He won't be satisfied with less than possessing you completely—body and soul. And when he's done with you, you will be empty inside, just as every other woman in his life has been. I cannot warn you about that strongly enough. He's not an entity to be trifled with. For the sake of your life, your soul—your very essence—keep him at a distance."

"Good night, Catherine."

"Don't ignore your dreams, Edwina. Truth comes out in dreams as your mind processes the things that you haven't been able to consciously accept."

"Even Freud said that a cigar was sometimes just a cigar, Catherine. Go away."

"Freud never studied your dreams. He had no acquaintance with a true prophet."

"Go away, Catherine," Edwina replied sharply.

"For now," the shade agreed. "But be very careful around him. He's extremely dangerous for you."

"I wish that you would stop being so cryptic and just say what you mean."

The spirit shook her head negatively. "I cannot. You would not believe me. There are times that you don't even believe that I am real, even though you see me quite clearly. I know that you sometimes believe that you are losing your mind when I appear to you. You definitely wouldn't believe me if I told you what sort of creature that entity is."

"Go away, Catherine."

"Listen to me, Edwina. I wasn't sent here for my good, but for your sake."

"Go away, Catherine. I don't believe a word of this. Leave me alone," Edwina said wearily. The last thing that Edwina considered herself was a prophet. She had dreams. Period. Some of which later came true. Some of which did not. Dreaming did not make one a prophet.

The shade winked out, but there was a defiant, ugly, expression on her face as she did so.

Edwina climbed out of bed and went to the kitchen. She looked at the clock. It was four forty-five in the morning. Her alarm clock would be going off in a little over an hour. She got herself a glass of cold water and went back to bed.

But she couldn't get back to sleep. She lay there thinking.

Who was Klaus von Bruner? Why had she dreamed of him for years? What did this all mean?

The rational part of her brain told her that this was all coincidental. Perhaps seen his photo once somewhere and had fixated upon him as the subject of her romantic fantasies. That's what any competent psychotherapist would have told her. Of course, they would have also told her that it was a sign of insanity to believe one's dreams. She didn't stand convinced of the truth of that position.

Too many of the things she had dreamed had later come true.

Sighing, she rolled over on her stomach, hit the pillow a couple of times and forced herself to relax. If she couldn't sleep, she'd at least rest. But she couldn't even do that.

She arose and went to the computer. Before she had put her dream journals into the safe deposit box at the bank, she had scanned them into the computer and uploaded them to the same area of a remote computer that she used for the storage of her research records. She had kept a copy of all the images on CD-ROM.

Downloading all the images from the remote storage site would take too long. She wasn't patient enough right now to do that. So, she took the first of the CD-ROMs and placed it in the drive.

The dreams about Klaus had gone back to her late childhood. The first drawing she had made of him had been when she had been ten. Her sketching skills then had been rather primitive. Yet the face was clearly Klaus'. She'd been dreaming of him for twenty-five years. He would have been in his late teens at the time she began drawing him. But this was not the face of a boy, but of a mature man. There were thousands of drawings of Klaus in her journals. Then there were drawings of places. There was an old Bavarian castle, a new Norman style stone house she thought was in an executive bracket U.S. subdivision, a villa she thought was in Italy, a *pied a terre* in Paris, a manor house in rural England, as well as a collection of other houses and apartments, all around the world.

She paused at a drawing she had made fifteen years before. It showed her in a lab with Klaus. Both of them were in lab coats. Klaus' sleeve was rolled up. There was a hypodermic in his hand. He was about to inject himself.

She read her notes about the dream. "Klaus has a substantially reduced ability to withstand UV radiation and a low ability to repair the damage from UV. Consequently, he only goes out at night or when he can be fully covered, especially his eyes, which are most sensitive. He has a severe iron deficiency warranting periodic units of blood to be given. Yet, he has an amazing ability to resist disease. His physical strength, endurance, and an ability to heal himself, in most situations, is beyond anything that I've ever encountered. The solution to the UV tolerance requires augmenting what little natural ability he has. The solution to augment his ability to repair the UV damage is more complicated. But, I believe it can be solved."

Then she had made three pages of research notes regarding potential solutions. All of which had been beyond her ability at the time of the dream. Much of what she had written—notes of her research journals in the dream—was then barely comprehensible to her given the scope of genetic engineering necessary to solve his problem. While she now understood the science, she was not at all sure it would work. She knew it to be a profoundly desperate act to even begin such research. The solution would either cure him or kill him. She wouldn't feel comfortable giving odds on which outcome would occur. It was dangerous to even think about creating a retrovirus to reprogram his DNA.

Edwina had long since forgotten about that particular dream. Yet, all of her research since then had been aimed more or less in this direction. She hadn't even realized that she had been preparing herself to undertake this work.

The question was: could human resistance to UV radiation be augmented through genetic engineering? She had begun similar work in plants, modifying the DNA controlling their UV tolerance in order to increase yields. If the work could be translated from plant to man, what would the ramifications be? Could the cure be worse than the disease? Or was she simply going off the deep end?

Even if the research could produce a solution to the problem, the work would take years, possibly decades or even a century. She suspected the solution would be that complicated. In the sketch, neither of them appeared much older than their current ages. It didn't make any sense.

She continued to click through the images. Several images later, she saw an image that she did recall. It was of a wedding, her wedding. The image label read "Mardi Gras wedding with Klaus' cousin, Father Wilhelm from the Vatican, as officiant." The groom was clearly Klaus. And the church was her current parish. However, until just before Thanksgiving of last year, she had never stepped foot in that building. Yet, this drawing was dated a good fourteen years prior. The sanctuary and nave had been remodeled only five years ago. The drawing clearly reflected the current decor. This sketch sent shivers down her spine.

A larger external chill at her back told her that Catherine was once more present.

"He's been invading your dreams for years, Edwina," the shade said quietly, "preparing you to accept him. Conditioning you, brainwashing you, so that you see him only in a favorable light, trying to influence your mind so that you are willing to do his bidding."

"No one can invade someone else's dreams," she dismissed sharply.

"But, then again, until you met me, you wouldn't have thought that spirits were real, either," Catherine offered and then faded away.

Edwina looked at the time display at the bottom of her computer monitor's screen. She sighed as the alarm clock went off. With the shop opening today, she didn't have time to go back to bed.

Chapter Three

Still in her robe, she recorded the growth on the plants in her greenhouse. This was going better than she had anticipated. But only maintaining the strain and improving it over several generations of plants would tell her if this genetic modification would be otherwise harmless and if the modification would stay true. The seeds for this generation, and for all the generations before it, were stored out at the landscape nursery in her office space, just in case anything happened to this experiment.

After she tended the plants, she dressed and walked down to the Church. Having some time before mass began she ducked into the traditional side of the confessional. She really needed to talk to someone. One of the priests was always there for an hour before each Mass. But she didn't think she could look any priest in the face and tell him about her reaction to Klaus without becoming too flustered for words.

"Bless me, Father, for I have sinned. It is has been six days since my last confession. In that time, I have willfully spoken a lie. I told a man I wasn't afraid of him, and yet I was—and am still—afraid. I have entertained impure thoughts and desires about this man. I have allowed those thoughts to become actions. It has gone no further than rather heavy petting, Father. That is due more to his self-control than mine. He's the one who had the strength to bring an end to the intimacy when I did not. For these sins and all those I may have forgotten, I beg forgiveness of God, and penance and absolution of you, Father."

From behind the screen, the priest said, "God gave us the gift of sexual desires for our good. The proper use of those desires is a good and wondrous thing, allowing people to share in the self-giving love of God, a love that is so real that the product of that love must be named and nurtured. Is there some reason existing to make the desire you feel for this man shameful? Is there any impediment to this relationship becoming a Christian marriage?"

"To the best of my knowledge, we are both free of impediments. I find it uncomfortable to think just how non-existent my self-control is around him."

From behind the screen, the priest said, "You're human. Cut yourself some slack. I absolve you in the name of the Father, and the Son, and the Holy Ghost. For your penance, you are to read the *Song of Songs*, thoughtfully, prayerfully. God gave us sexual desires for his own purposes — for the mutual joy of man and woman as well as for the procreation of children to be brought up in the love of God."

He continued, "Keep the purposes of God in mind, try always to be a means of grace for the man in your life, and be open to letting him be a means of grace for you. In the best of marriages, each partner will seek the other's good before their own. Now go in peace."

Returning from church after Mass, she made herself some breakfast and changed into the "uniform" for the shop — a long dark skirt, white cotton blouse, and cameo. The idea was to reinforce the Victorian theme. Then she opened her old Vulgate Bible and did her penance. It had been a long time since she had read this particular book of poetry. It had been quite a while since she had read Latin at all, but it came back to her rapidly.

When she got to chapter eight, she stopped and reread verses six and seven. She translated it as:

"Wear me as a seal upon your heart, wear me as a seal upon your arm, for love is as cruel as death, and passion hard as the grave, the lamps thereof are fire and flame. Many waters cannot quench love, neither can the floods drown it – if a man should give all the substance of his house for love, he shall despise the cost as nothing."

Would she despise it as nothing, to give everything that she had for Klaus' love? She smiled at that thought and knew that she would count whatever the cost of having him in her life as something minimal.

Finishing the book of poetry, she closed the Bible.

* * * * *

Edwina opened up the shop at eleven that morning, right on schedule. The garden shop was open for business a grand total of ten minutes when the fax machine spit out an order. Edwina looked at it. Herr Doctor von Bruner decided that he had to have that set of patio furniture that he had looked at last evening as well as a pair of granite bird baths. He wanted them delivered by six in the evening.

It was a substantial order. She figured it up, deducted his credit, then she processed his charge card for the difference. She couldn't afford to turn down business, even if the order was a transparent ploy for him to ingratiate himself with her. However, if Herr Doctor von Bruner thought that she would deliver this to him herself, he was doomed to deep and profound disappointment.

First, the pieces were far too heavy for Edwina to manage without assistance. Second, she wasn't about to be ordered about by that man. She called the delivery service.

Beginning around noon, the traffic through the shop was relatively heavy. Mostly that was due to the Grand Opening drawings. People will come out in droves to get something for nothing. The slips that were placed in the hopper would give the shop a good start at a mass mailing list of those interested in garden products. The people who came through the shop weren't all looking exclusively for freebies. She managed to move quite a bit of merchandise. Edwina also booked a number of appointments for consultations on garden design. Things were beginning to work out. She might actually be able to make a go of this, as something besides a hobby. Only time would tell.

The store was scheduled to close at nine that evening. It was eight forty-five when he walked in.

Tonight he wasn't wearing evening clothes, but an obviously hand-tailored dark blue worsted wool business suit, a fine white linen shirt with a tasteful silk tie and tie pin set with a very nice diamond, along with handmade Italian leather shoes. The shirt had French cuffs—the old fashioned kind that closed with links instead of buttons. His cuff links were also gold set with diamonds. From the top of his five hundred dollar hair cut to the soles of his five thousand dollar handmade Italian shoes, his appearance proclaimed him to be profoundly old money.

He had been formidable in evening clothes. He was no more approachable in business wear. Yet, Edwina knew that he would have drawn any woman's attention, whatever he was—or wasn't—wearing. Klaus von Bruner was, as he was all too well aware, an incredibly attractive man.

She completed her dealings with the pair of customers she was assisting before she spoke with him. "Good evening, Herr von Bruner."

He smiled at her. It was a smile guaranteed to melt the heart of any woman.

She wasn't any more immune to his charms tonight than she had been yesterday. It frightened her just how susceptible to him she was.

"That uniform reinforces the Victorian theme quite nicely," he said commenting upon the long dark skirt and white cotton blouse, which was worn with an antique cameo at the throat. "Quite nicely indeed, with your lovely auburn hair upswept like that. You could have easily stepped out of the pages of any number of Victorian fashion plates."

"Not precisely. I categorically refuse to cinch in my waist to sixteen inches, nor will I have ribs surgically removed to facilitate such a constriction. There is a reason why fainting couches were so popular among the Victorians. Women couldn't get a substantial enough breath to maintain any level of activity if they were at all concerned with fashion."

"History is also an area of study you have pursued?"

"To a minor extent. How may I serve you this evening?"

He smiled again. She really wished he wouldn't do that. His smile filled her head with entirely too many thoughts of throwing herself into his arms, too many remembrances about the feel and taste of his mouth, too many thoughts of locking up and taking him upstairs and to her lonely bed. No, the man was entirely too tempting, she decided. Yet, Edwina couldn't stop looking at him. She couldn't stop thinking about him. She chided herself for this adolescent behavior. For heaven's sake, she was thirty-five, not some silly boy-crazy teenager recently allowed free from the strictures of a convent boarding school.

He finally spoke. "I wish to be rid of the large expanse of grass in the back of my home and establish a true garden. I can think of no one whose judgment I would rely upon more than I would yours."

She opened her appointment book. "When would be a good time for me to come out to walk it off and take soil samples?"

"Tonight would be lovely."

"Sorry. I need to see the grounds by daylight."

He smiled again. "A gentleman might think that you did not trust him."

"A gentleman would not ask a lady to his home on such short acquaintance."

Klaus nodded once. "In a perfect world, Edwina, what you say is true. I have a feeling that you are hiding behind outdated conventions merely because you do not trust me."

"I do not know you well enough to trust you."

He spoke in rapid German. "You are refreshing, Edwina. Seldom, people are so blunt with me."

"I fear I know far more about *Dendrobrium Nobile*, *Angelica Archangelica*, or even *Mammiliaria Muehlenpfordtii* than I do about tactfulness," she replied in English.

"Orchids, herbs, and cacti," he observed thoughtfully. "Quite a spread of knowledge."

"And you have some background in botany."

"Pharmacological, not horticultural," he dismissed. "I have, however, been reading several books on garden design of late in an effort to decide what to do with all that grass at the back of my home. The lawn is the bane of my existence. I hate it with a grand passion."

She chuckled and smiled. "You amuse me."

"On account of my hatred of grass?"

"Of course."

"Why should this amuse you?"

"You sound so much like my father. He also detested vast expanses of manicured lawn. Mostly, I suspect because he hated the work in maintaining it."

"Wise man, indeed, your father."

"He was also a perfectionist of the first order," she stated quietly before warning, "I am very much like him."

Klaus nodded. "I can believe that. Now, it is well past closing time. Would you walk down the street with me to the restaurant on the corner and have dinner?"

"Only if it is a business dinner, not a social evening. We can discuss your specifications for your garden. Of course, you must allow me to pay for the meal, as a business expense. IRS still allows business dinners as a deductible item."

He frowned slightly.

She found that she far preferred his smiles.

"Independent, aren't you?" he asked quietly. But the tone held no rancor. It was simply a statement of reality.

"That is one of the nicer epithets to ever be used to describe me. Generally, 'bloody-minded' is a more commonly used epithet. I've also been called 'mule-headed', 'stubborn', 'inflexible', and 'immovable'. Those are some of the nicer names. If this is to be a business dinner, I will certainly be happy to sit and discuss your garden. I haven't eaten since early this morning, and find that I am suddenly quite hungry."

He smiled. "Is the restaurant down the street on the corner acceptable?"

"Bill and Beth always serve a good meal in a relaxed atmosphere. We should be able to discuss your garden there."

She gathered her soft-sided brief case and a coat before she locked up.

As they walked down to the restaurant, he offered her his arm. She smiled at him as she placed her hand on his forearm. The evening was brisk, verging on downright cold.

Suddenly, he asked, "If you could have anything in the world, anything at all, what would you wish for?"

That question took her a bit aback. "Anything? Anything within the realm of that which exists? Or anything regardless of impossibility?"

"Anything. Anything at all. It doesn't at all matter how wild, impossible, or improbable it may be. What would you wish for?"

She sighed. "There is no question in my mind. I would want to have dinner with my parents just once more. I should like to spend a quiet winter's evening at home with them. I would like to discuss music with my mother, to play another game of chess with my father, and to spend a couple of hours with them playing music once more. Mother taught music. Father was a talented amateur musician. He was a mathematician by profession. He always said that music was math in sound. Above all things, I'd like to have just one more winter's evening with them."

"I take it that they are no longer alive?"

"They died two years ago in a car crash."

"I'm sorry."

She shook her head slightly and sighed. "I'd called them on the morning of the crash and we'd talked for a few minutes. When they died, they were on their way to the airport to catch a plane to New York, and then to London. Mother always loved London. Father was taking her there as an anniversary present. They never even made it to the airport. They were dead at the scene of the accident. I miss them terribly." She blinked back tears. "Pretty silly wish, huh?"

"No," he said gently as they approached the restaurant, "I do not think it silly in the least. Time and family are two items that all the money in the world cannot purchase. If we are truly blessed, we might be able to give the best of those things we received from our parents to the next generation."

She sighed. "If we are that blessed," she agreed.

"You like children?"

Edwina smiled. "Yes. I used to want a big family."

"Then why haven't you married?"

She sighed. Then she smiled and said in a tone she hoped that he'd take for teasing, "I suppose that's because you haven't asked me."

Klaus smiled. "That can be easily enough remedied. What would your reply be if I were to ask?"

"I couldn't possibly speculate on that."

"Why not?"

"I refuse to deal in hypothetical questions. If you want an answer to a question, you will have to ask me directly. I may or may not answer. Indirect questions are merely annoying."

"What instruments do you play?" he asked, changing the subject.

Edwina felt a keen sense of disappointment at his change of subject. "I play several stringed instruments...violin, cello, and guitar."

"Guitar?"

She smiled at the disbelief in his voice. She couldn't contain the chuckle.

"What do you find humorous?" he demanded.

"Your reaction. As an undergraduate, I played in a rock band. The band provided a bit of mad money, as well as an outlet for my excess energy and as such the band kept me out of trouble."

"You were, of course, otherwise in grave danger of finding yourself in trouble," he added dryly.

"You have no idea."

"My, what secrets of yours I am learning," he replied thoughtfully.

They reached the restaurant door. Klaus held the door.

"That's me," Edwina dismissed with a large measure of irony, "Woman of mystery."

"You think, perhaps, you are not?" he demanded softly.

"My life is an open book, an open rather boring book at that."

He looked at her in blatant disbelief. "Hardly," he dismissed. "I would hardly say that your life was either an open book, or a boring one. In fact, you fascinate me. But, I believe I have told you that before now."

The restaurant was mostly empty. The dinner crowd had mostly come and gone. The bar crowd, however, was in full force on this Saturday night.

They took a table well away from the bar. One of the owners was over to the table immediately.

"What's good tonight, Beth?"

Beth smiled broadly. "I thought about saving you a wonderful steak in honor of your Grand Opening celebration, Edwina. Knowing you, I saved you some terrific fresh salmon. We sold a lot of it tonight. However, I'm certain that there are two filets left, for you and your gentleman friend."

"Klaus?" Edwina asked. "What would you like?"

"Fish is fine."

"If you would rather have a steak, or anything else, please don't feel confined by my selections," Edwina offered.

"I rather like fish, actually," Klaus said gently.

She smiled at Beth. "Then we'll both have the salmon."

Beth nodded. "Anything else?"

"I feel like celebrating. Tell Bill I want a bottle of his best champagne with dessert. I'll trust him on the vintage."

Then Edwina turned to her companion, "Klaus, have you a preference of wine with dinner?"

He named an excellent German wine, extremely expensive, but worth every penny. Klaus' eyes sparkled with mischief. Oh, how she was growing fond of that man, in spite of herself.

Beth thought for a moment. "I know that we had six bottles of that in the cellar at the beginning of the evening. I know that we sold at least four of them. I need to check to see if there is any left. I'll be back in a few moments."

"Does she really stock that wine?" Klaus asked lowly.

Edwina nodded in the affirmative. "I've had a tour of their wine cellar. It is truly impressive."

"Do you not eat red meat?" he asked. "The waitress said that she was going to save you a steak, but instead kept back the fish."

"I generally allow myself red meat only on Sundays. Most of the time, I eat either vegetarian fare, chicken, or fish."

"Out of health concerns?" he asked carefully.

"No. It's a personal discipline."

"Many people have no discipline in their lives, allowing themselves every indulgence they imagine they deserve."

"Self-control is not fashionable, these days," Edwina said.

"Self-control never has been fashionable. Somehow, I do not believe that you would ever be one to allow a little thing such as fashion dictate your actions. I strongly suspect that you will always do what you believe to be correct regardless of either what anyone else thinks or any unfavorable consequences."

"I should hope so. "

Bill, Beth's husband, came out of the back with a bottle of the wine Klaus had ordered. She watched as they went through the inspection ritual. Klaus smiled and spoke a soft word of praise in German.

Bill poured two glasses of the wine. "Beth will be right out with your soup."

Klaus looked at her. "Surely, it is not just the two of them running this establishment? Or are we getting special treatment?"

"You have something against being cosseted and spoiled?"

"Not at all," he assured her with another of his heart melting smiles. "I surround myself with people whose jobs are to make my life run more smoothly, to cosset and spoil me. I rather like the feeling, actually."

"I did have that impression," she allowed.

"What other impressions have I made upon you?"

Edwina felt her face grow warm. She knew that she was blushing.

He smiled. "The question embarrasses you?"

"Yes. The answers may not be what you want to hear."

He looked at her for a long moment. "And what do you think I want to hear?"

"I do not believe that this subject is appropriate for a business discussion."

He smiled again. "You would prefer to stay with safer topics."

"Definitely."

"I never would have pegged you as a coward, Edwina."

She sipped her wine. "Then again, you don't know me very well."

"That will change."

"Awfully confident of that, aren't you?"

"I am. Back to the matter of the restaurant, then, why are we receiving special treatment?"

"Most of the dining room staff leaves at nine," she explained. "The dinner crowd is mostly gone by then. I come in fairly frequently at this time of night. The food here is quite good. Once they discovered that I had purchased the building down the block, Bill and Beth have treated me like family."

Beth laughed as she placed before them deep soup plates filled with the house homemade broccoli soup, that was quickly followed by a basket of hot whole-wheat rolls, and a supply of fresh butter. "Actually, we treat her better than family, as family gets put to work," the restaurateur confessed with a smile. "Now, Enjoy the soup," she said in her normal friendly voice before she departed, leaving them to discuss the matter of their business.

"You do not lease the shop?" Klaus asked as he dipped his spoon into the soup.

"No. I bought the building outright. The seller was quite motivated, it seemed. For a cash deal, he was willing to take less than the half the market value of the building. The tenants along the street provide a fairly sizable income independent of my shop. I have a wonderful open space upstairs, which is virtually soundproofed from the tenants beneath, much of that space, I have converted to greenhouse. The rest I use for living and office space. Generally, I like it."

"Greenhouse? What do you grow?"

She hesitated. "I have a section dedicated to my orchids. Then I have a section of herbs. I grow most of my own fresh vegetables."

"Then you have given up your research," Klaus observed.

"I am constantly posing questions to myself and needing to find the answers."

"What could motivate someone to take a loss of that magnitude on a building," Klaus asked, changing the subject.

"The building is alleged to be haunted."

"*Haunted*?" Klaus asked with sharp interest. "As in ghosts?"

Edwina shrugged. "That is the generally accepted meaning of the word. According to my tenants, or rather according to one of my tenants, there are several rather unpleasant spirits in the building."

"Do you believe this?" he asked softly.

"Let's just say that I am still gathering data. I've been there for two months, and I've yet to see or hear anything even remotely malevolent, apart from one of my tenants who rather decidedly gives me the creeps."

"Perhaps the tenant's claim to hauntings has to do with the fact he wished to buy the building?"

She shrugged. "I can't be certain of that. I don't believe he could raise the necessary funds to buy the building. It is my strong suspicion that the man is simply unbalanced. I do not think he is quite clinically insane. However, he is most definitely different."

"Doesn't that worry you?" Klaus asked.

"He pays his rent on time. Aside from his complaints about what he calls 'poltergeists', he is not a terrible tenant."

"You do not believe him to be dangerous, then?"

"I don't know him to be dangerous. And I'll continue to give him the benefit of doubt until or unless he makes me believe otherwise."

"Do you suspect that he could be dangerous?"

"Let's just say I go way out of my way not to spend time in his company."

"Are you afraid of him?"

"I am afraid of very few people, Klaus."

"Am I among that select few?" Klaus asked hesitantly.

"I am not afraid of you—cautious, yes—afraid, no. I am quite certain that you are a powerful man, powerful both physically and financially. I am absolutely certain that you have an agenda you are pursuing in my regard. I am also absolutely certain that your coming into the shop last evening was not in any way an accidental encounter."

His smile wavered just a bit before his eyes twinkled in mischief. "Guilty as charged on all counts. I throw myself on your tender mercy," he said in rapid German.

"That is a profoundly dangerous thing to do. I am not known to be overly merciful," she warned in his language. "Are you certain that you wish to put yourself at hazard?"

He chuckled in amusement. "A small measure of danger adds spice to life."

"Whereas a large measure gives indigestion?" she asked in English.

"At minimum," he agreed easily.

"Shall I tell you more of which I am certain?" she asked quietly after she took another sip of the wine. At his nod, she continued, "I am certain that you have excellent taste in wine. This is very nice. Thank you for ordering it."

"Your company is far more pleasant than the wine, Edwina," he told her quietly.

She took another spoonful of the soup and a bite of the roll. The food was, as usual, wonderful.

"Empty flattery will only make me angry," she warned. "Suppose that we discuss the matter of your garden, unless that was simply a ruse to get me here?"

"Just how many plays ahead in chess do you think?"

"That would depend on how well I know my opponent. The better I know the thought processes of my opponent, the more moves I am able to anticipate."

"Then I shall very much enjoy the day that you are able to state that you know me quite well."

"I wonder if anyone truly knows you that well," she stated, thinking aloud.

He was taken aback by that comment. "You may well be correct," he admitted quietly. "I am said to be most formidable."

"Now, that I do believe. I cannot see you suffering fools gladly. Yet, I do not find you particularly formidable."

He smiled at her. "I do not wish for you to find me so."

"Yet, I do imagine that you could be truly distant and unapproachable if you wished to be."

"No more than you yourself can be so," he countered. "Your reputation is rather at odds with the woman I have discovered you to be."

"And just what is my reputation?" she asked hesitantly.

"Brilliant mind, profoundly logical and yet able to think outside of conventions, coldly efficient, completely asexual, acerbic tongued with an absolutely wicked ability to flay an opponent without as much as raising her gentle voice, a distant perfectionist driving herself and all those around her to high achievement, all in all a difficult person to manage. But a very good person to give an assignment and stay out of her way while she completes it."

She sipped the wine. "That last bit is as good a distillation of my personality as any, I suppose. In what areas do you see variance?"

"You are a vibrant woman, hardly the colorless lab rat I was led to expect," he said quietly.

She laughed boldly as she reached for her sketchpad from within her brief case. "A colorless lab rat... Oh, dear, that is a mental picture I shall carry for a long time. Oh, that is priceless. Thank you." She took a pencil in hand and then began sketching. He sat there and enjoyed his soup, wondering what she was sketching.

When she was done a few minutes later, she handed him the sketch. It was quickly done, but there was definitely nothing amateurish about it. The sketch was of Edwina as a rat. Her face was on the body of a rat that was standing on its hind legs. A long lab coat was buttoned up to the throat.

"Is that what you thought of me?" she teased.

He nodded negatively as he handed her back the sketch. "Hardly. There is nothing of the lab rat in you. Neither is there anything remotely asexual about you. You are one hundred percent profoundly desirable, passionate, woman. Any man who could describe you as asexual has to have something seriously wrong with his senses."

She felt her face grow warm. "Perhaps," she allowed after sipping her wine.

He shook his head negatively. "No perhaps about it, Edwina. You are the most desirable woman I have ever known."

She nodded negatively. "Right," she dismissed.

"You do not believe me?"

"I am thirty-five years old, Klaus. In all that time, I've never noticed that I was capable of inspiring that degree of desire in any man, let alone a man like you who could have any woman he wants."

"You are the only woman I want," Klaus said.

"For now."

"Forever. I am at a loss as to why you have been described as asexual."

"In the lab, I purposefully cultivate that asexual attitude. I don't care to be propositioned by my coworkers."

"By whom do you care to be propositioned?"

"You have this marked ability to pose immensely personal questions."

"Yes. I do. Will you answer that question?"

She changed the subject rapidly. "No. I don't believe I will. Tell me what you want from your garden, Klaus. First, how much ground is involved?"

He sipped his wine then smiled. "I like the sound of my name on your lips, Edwina. Please continue to use it. By the way, no one had said anything to me about your artistic ability. You are quite a good sketch artist."

She shrugged, "I manage well enough to do what I need to do. But, I'm not an artist. A couple of my cousins got most of the artistic ability in the family. I am an adequate technical illustrator and cartoonist. Not much more," she answered.

"You're entirely too modest."

"Just honest."

He smiled at her. "I can see that it's going to be interesting to get to know you."

"How much ground is involved in the proposed garden?"

"The garden area will be about six acres," he replied after a moment.

She had to laugh. Somehow, she doubted this man ever did anything on a small scale. She didn't know why a six acre garden surprised her. But it did. "Six acres?" she echoed.

A furrow formed between his brows as he obviously redid the calculations.

"You think in metric measurements, don't you?" she observed.

He nodded. "It is sometimes difficult to force myself to move between systems of measurements."

"I understand. The size of your garden is six acres?"

"Yes. Six acres, more or less, is the size of the garden. The stables and exercise yard for my horses takes up three acres. The house, pool, tennis courts, and garage take up an acre. It's a ten acre plot, more or less, on which the house sits."

"What is on the acreage now?"

"Virtually nothing. Grass. A mortared fieldstone fence around the perimeter. Some immature oak and maple trees. Nothing of much significance or interest," he dismissed.

"Tell me what you want from the acreage."

"I prefer formal gardens. I like knot gardens and topiary."

"Good topiary takes years, Klaus."

"I'm not planning on leaving the States anytime soon, aside from brief business trips."

"What else do you want from the garden?"

"There should always be color regardless of the season. The only time that I have to be in the garden is in the evenings. I'd prefer some night blooming varieties so that I could have full enjoyment of the garden."

"Okay. I càn probably arrange that."

"If I could, I would like a section of herb garden done in the Victorian style. And I should like a small orchard of fruit trees and berry vines—apples, pears, cherries, apricots, peaches, figs, kiwi—as well as strawberries, blueberries, boysenberries, gooseberries, and blackberries. Oh, and a patch of asparagus. I am quite fond of asparagus in the early spring."

Edwina smiled. "The soil requirements for several of those plants are radically different from what the others require."

"You'll manage."

"What else do you want?"

"There is one section of ground near the house that is lower than the rest. It would be perfect place for a hidden garden, a private retreat. I should like to have it separated off from the rest with trellised roses. I like roses. "

"Is that why you purchased the furniture, for this private retreat?"

"It is."

"The type of garden that you have described leaves no place in which for children to run and play."

"Like you, *Fraulein*, I am unmarried," he told her in German.

She couldn't keep the relieved smile from crossing her face.

He looked at her for a long moment. "You are smiling. The fact that I am a bachelor pleases you. That is most encouraging," he continued in German.

"I would hardly have thought that you would need encouragement from me," she replied in his language.

"Where you are concerned, yes, I rather think that I need quite a massive dose of encouragement," he stated quietly in English.

"The kind of garden you desire will be profoundly high maintenance," she warned, in English, changing the subject back to business. "The costs of keeping it in order will be high."

He smiled at her again. "You offer garden maintenance services, do you not? Surely, any maintenance arrangements can be worked out."

Definitely, he was trying to ingratiate himself with her. She ate a bit more of the soup. "They can. How much of a budget were you thinking of for the establishment of the gardens?"

"Whatever it takes, up to five hundred thousand."

She wasn't going to bat an eye at that. The kind of garden he wanted would not be inexpensive, especially if specimen sized plantings were to be involved. Granted she would get most of the plantings from the landscape nursery at far less than retail. But she still had to give her nursery partner her fair share. "Five hundred thousand. Hmmm… I might be able to bring it in for that. Assuming of course that we are talking US Dollars, not Euro, nor Deutschmarks."

"Dollars."

"Frankly, it could take every bit of that to do a garden of that size, just in the cost of specimen sized plants," she warned. "My design fee for this complex of a design is ten thousand dollars. Then there will be the cost of the plants and the labor."

He took out his checkbook. He wrote the check and handed it to her. "And how long do you anticipate the project to take?"

"You just hand out checks like this without a contract?" Edwina demanded.

"I trust you."

"You don't know me."

"I know you well enough to know that I will get every penny of my money's worth from your design. You are an honorable woman. How long do you anticipate the project to take?"

She sighed. "It will not be an overnight project, Klaus. Give me the address. I'll come out on Monday morning, walk it off, take some photos, bring out my crew chief, and we'll begin to work out the design. I should have some preliminary thoughts for you by a week from today."

"Monday. Not tomorrow?"

"I do not personally do servile work on Sunday. Ever. It is just another way in which I am profoundly old-fashioned and difficult to work with."

"Your reputation rankles somewhat, does it not?"

"It does. I don't go out of my way to be difficult to people."

"No. I can see that you do not. Having come to meet you, I find much of your reputation unfounded. Oh, you are brilliant, unquestionably. I would agree that you are efficient. I can see that you have the clear ability to flay a man's skin at four hundred paces with just a word if you would find that necessary. I would not call you either cold or asexual, reserved, perhaps. Yet that is not even correct. Perhaps 'formal' would be more accurate. In an informal society, formality, living according to rules of behavior, can be seen as decidedly odd. However, there is nothing wrong with choosing to live one's life following time-honored rules of honor."

"Nothing, except that most people fail to recognize that there are rules," she offered quietly. "Let alone that following the rules could make life flow more smoothly for themselves and for their families. I suppose that I do put people off by insisting on certain standards of behavior for myself and others in their interactions with me."

"Any type of nonconformity tends to see one labeled as odd."

"True."

"Very well, Edwina. If you will not work on Sunday, then I shall leave word with the staff to expect you on Monday morning," he said as he handed her his business card. "The address is accurate."

"You will not be there?"

He shook his head negatively. "Unfortunately, I shall be dealing with my sister, Karen, and doing several video-conferences on Monday. " His voice was full of brotherly amusement.

"Is Karen your only sister?" Edwina asked.

"No. There were four of us — three sisters and myself."

"And you were the eldest, so you had the duty to protect them."

He nodded. "Yes, I am the eldest."

"Your sisters are all in their thirties, then?"

"More signs of interest in me. I'm forty-one years old, Edwina. Do you care to know anything else about me?"

She felt her face grow warm again. "What do you want to tell me?"

"I think if I told you everything that I wished to tell you, I fear that you would run away from me like a frightened rabbit."

"I'm rather enjoying the evening. I should hate for it to end one moment before it must. So, if some statement would spoil the rather mellow tenor of the evening, please don't say it."

"Very well. We will need to have that conversation sooner or later."

"If it is to be unpleasant, then the later, the better."

He smiled. "When you have something to tell me about the garden, Edwina, call me or send me a sketch of the design by fax. However, should you ever desire simply to speak with me, then please call. I will leave word that you are to be put through immediately."

As Edwina saw Beth coming over, she decided to wait to reply. Beth cleared away the soup plates and advised them, "The salmon will be out in two minutes."

"Thanks, Beth," Edwina told her friend.

When Beth had retreated, Edwina looked at Klaus and warned, "Putting this much money into the house, you have to know that you will be pricing it well over the market."

"I plan to live there for several more years. For the immediate future, I plan on staying in America."

"If you married an American citizen, you could remain here indefinitely," she offered in German after a brief silence. She didn't want to think that Klaus was pursuing her for the sake of easing an immigration problem. But it wouldn't be the first time that something like that happened to an American woman.

Klaus just looked at her in disbelief as Beth set their dinner plates before them.

The salmon looked wonderful. It was Beth's recipe. The baked fish was encrusted with a combination of crushed macadamia nuts and several herbs from Edwina's own greenhouse. It was served with fresh asparagus spears and a wild rice pilaf with almond slivers.

"Thank you, Beth. It looks wonderful," Edwina told her.

Klaus took a bite of his fish. He nodded. "It is wonderful," he told Beth.

The restaurateur smiled and walked away.

"Edwina," he asked lowly in a tone of disbelief, "Is a Green Card the reason you think I am pursuing you?"

"The thought had crossed my mind."

"As long as all it did was cross your mind. I would hate for an erroneous notion like that to take up residence in that lovely head of yours. I have absolutely no problems with Immigration and Naturalization. Nor do I anticipate having any."

"Why are you chasing me, Klaus? There is no doubt in my mind that you have decided to pursue me for more than my professional capabilities as a garden designer."

He rolled his eyes. "I always thought I had such a way with women," he said mostly to himself.

"It's the combination of your handsome face, healthy bank account, and the air of European nobility. You must be used to mercenary women falling at your feet."

He looked at her for a long time before speaking. "In my younger days, that was true enough. Few of the women could hold my attention for long. I am a difficult man, my dear."

"In your younger days...You are hardly ancient, Klaus. You are no child, but you are not Methuselah, either."

He was quiet for a long time. "There are days I feel every moment of my age," he said quietly, breaking the silence between them. Then he smiled broadly. "You are also not a child. There must have been men who have chased you at one time or other. Have you never been tempted to let one of them catch you?"

"There haven't been that many men who've ever seriously tried to catch me. Besides, I've always been a rather swift runner."

"You aren't running all that swiftly now," he challenged.

"I'm thirty five, Klaus. At this age, a woman thinks seriously from time to time of marrying and raising children, if she meets the right man."

"Am I the right man?"

"I don't know. Time, I suppose, will tell."

"I shall work on that reference from someone you know and trust."

She smiled at him. "Do that."

"May I call you?"

"I'd be disappointed if you didn't," she admitted before she took another bite of the salmon.

"I shall remember this restaurant. The food and service is marvelous."

"Wait until you see their desserts. They make them all in-house."

"What's their specialty?"

"Anything chocolate."

Klaus smiled. "Of course."

"How are you difficult?" Edwina asked him, going back to his previous statement.

"There are those among my employees who would reply to that with the question 'How is he not difficult?'"

"I once interviewed with your corporation."

"So, I am aware. Why didn't you accept the offer that was made to you? Was the money insufficient? Are the benefits not to your liking?"

"I couldn't get a written guarantee that I could do the work I wanted to do. I strongly feel that my life is too short to be pigeonholed into work in which I have no interest. But, then again, that is another way in which I am, myself, difficult."

He sighed. "There is a job for you at the corporation in our research department doing the work you want to do whenever you want it. All you have to do is tell me that you want it. Human Resources was instructed to make you the offer of underwriting your personal research. I am profoundly disappointed that they failed to do so."

"Why?"

"I've read your dissertations. I've read your publications. You would be a valuable addition to any research team. I have to admit I was more than merely surprised when you opened the shop instead of continuing to do your research."

She only smiled at him.

Klaus returned the smile. "Ah. You didn't abandon the work. You are still doing your research. Are you working alone?"

"If I were working, it would be alone."

"Still working on maximizing the therapeutic yield of narcotics through manipulating the genetic code?"

She shrugged. "I haven't confirmed that I am working on any research."

"I understand. However, what I don't understand is why someone would walk away from a well-equipped, well-funded, well-staffed lab in order to undertake research on her own."

"I'd say a researcher might have left and knocked the dust off her feet because the people managing of that lab were categorically stupid and short sighted."

"That doesn't explain why that same brilliant scientist wouldn't have gone to work for another company."

"The scientist may be barred by her previous contract from continuing that work with any other company for a period of time."

"That would do it. Aren't you afraid they'll finish your work?"

"The researchers remaining with my former company are competent lab technicians, but not terribly imaginative. I doubt that any of them will have the insight necessary to carry on the work I left behind. It requires several intuitive leaps which are somewhat beyond them."

He smiled. "Did you sabotage your records there, by any chance?"

"No. I didn't sabotage anything. That would be unethical. It's just that I tend to keep my personal research notes in a rather intense code that few people, or few computers, have ever been able to decipher."

"I see," he said with a smile.

"The research is pretty well dead in the water, there."

"What are you working on, if not the previous project?"

"I haven't confirmed that I'm working on anything."

"A scientist working by herself has to be difficult, slow, and expensive."

"It would be, if one opted to pursue that avenue."

"Would it go faster with a couple of assistants and a research grant?"

She shrugged. "Probably. But I'm sure that any scientist would be handling this fine on her own. And I'm equally sure that this scientist would rather keep things under wraps until she had publishable results."

"You won't accept a grant? I have grant research monies going unclaimed. You might as well have them."

She shook her head negatively. "I will keep the offer in mind if I'm ever in the situation where I need research monies, thank you."

"You are independent, aren't you?" he replied, his voice puzzled.

Clearly, she thought, he had never had anyone turn down money from him.

"I had thought that we had settled that matter of my independence earlier this evening."

He smiled. "You do your research in your apartment greenhouse?"

"You are certainly interested in this mythical research," she observed quietly.

"I am."

"The ostensible reason for this dinner was to discuss your garden. Or is the garden merely another hypothetical matter?"

"No. It's real enough. But the garden was only an excuse."

She felt her face grow warm again. "Klaus…"

"Do you know how rare it is to find a grown woman who can still blush in this day and age?" Klaus asked lowly.

"It's just another way in which I am out of touch with the modern world. Besides, with my coloring, I'm apt to blush boldly until I'm ninety. Red heads often do."

Klaus smiled at her. "You'll still be beautiful when you are ninety."

She returned the smile. "I suspect that I will be a good deal like my grandmother. Heaven help the world."

"I hear affection in your voice. You are fond of your grandmother."

"Grandmother is... well... you'd have to know her. She is extraordinary."

"If she is anything like her granddaughter, I'd have to agree with that assessment."

They spoke about his garden for most of the rest of the evening.

Of course, she picked up the bill for dinner. It was astronomical. But then again, they weren't cheap wines that they had been drinking. Edwina added a fifteen percent tip to the credit card slip. The thought was sobering that the tip was more than she normally spent on groceries in a week. But this was business.

Then he walked her back to the shop. She'd had more to drink this evening than she was used to, so she was feeling a little giddy. She wasn't falling down drunk. But she was definitely on the happy side of the spectrum.

"Thank you for the lovely meal," Klaus said quietly.

"Thank you for the opportunity to design your garden."

He smiled at her. "Are you going to invite me in, Edwina?"

"No. I don't know you well enough to be alone with you, especially when I've been drinking."

"Not quite as iron-willed as you pretend to be?"

"I don't pretend anything. I'm simply following good advice and avoiding occasions of sin."

"There's another old-fashioned Catholic term."

"I'm a rather old-fashioned Catholic lady, in case you haven't figured that one out."

"So, I'm an occasion of sin for you? I'd rather be an occasion of grace."

"Perhaps, you might yet be. Perhaps we both might be an occasion of grace for one another. Goodnight, Klaus. Thank you for a lovely evening."

"Dream of me, Edwina."

"Is that an order?" she demanded.

"A request," he said quietly as he stepped closer and touched her face. "A humble request."

"I doubt that you've ever been humble in your whole life."

"I have never been in any danger of being truthfully accused of such," he admitted dryly. "I'm a bit on the proud and overbearing side."

Edwina giggled. "No," she protested falsely. "I never would have noticed."

"Neither have I ever been truthfully accused of missing opportunities," he said lowly, his voice thick with passion. "And I'm not about to miss this one." Then he kissed her.

Just as the night before, he was devouring her. She was letting him. Letting him? Aiding and abetting him, was more like it. Returning passion for passion was more accurate.

There was more than need here. There was tenderness. There was love. Even in her befuddled state, she was aware of this. Whatever else was going on, there was love growing between the two of them. She cared for this man. And she knew that he cared for her.

"Enough," she reluctantly said as she found the strength to step back from him, even though that was the last thing she wanted to do. "No more, Klaus. Please. I'm at the edge of my control."

He smiled at her. "Control has its place Edwina, my dearest, but that place is not when you are in my arms," he said. "After we've been wed for fifty years, I will still want you as I do now."

She looked at him for a long moment. "Did you just say what I thought you said?" she asked, her voice shaking.

"I did. Marry me, Edwina. We'll fly to Reno tonight. I have a house on the lake there. It's beautiful. You will enjoy it."

She sighed. It wasn't a question. He actually expected her to fly half way across the country to marry him in a civil ceremony tonight. She smiled. "We'll talk about it sometime when my head isn't spinning from a combination of wine and your kiss. It's definitely a heady combination."

"But, you won't marry me tonight?"

"No, Klaus. When I marry, if I marry, I intend to do that in Church with my family and friends around me. I plan on only marrying once in my life. We have so much that we need to learn about one another before we even contemplate marriage."

"Like what?"

"Are you Catholic?"

"I am. My family has always been Catholic back all the way to the sixth century."

"That's good. At least, we both have reasonably the same expectations about marriage."

"Very well. We'll arrange a Church wedding."

"I didn't say that I'd marry you."

"Won't you?"

"Probably."

He smiled. "Walk with me, Edwina. I don't want you to go from me, yet."

"It's a little chilly to be taking the air, Klaus."

"Then come for a drive with me. The car will be warm."

"Are you driving?"

"Schmidt drives. We can sit behind the privacy glass and talk."

"Talk?"

"Or make love."

"Aren't we a little old to be making love in a car?" she teased.

"Ever tried it?"

She looked over her eyeglasses at him.

"You don't intimidate me."

"That's good."

"Come for a drive with me. It would be a new experience for you."

Edwina couldn't help but laugh. "You are a new experience for me. I wouldn't want to be overwhelmed by too many new experiences all at once."

"I take it, then, that this is goodnight?"

"Yes. Goodnight, Klaus."

He kissed her forehead and took the keys out of her hand. He unlocked the door and turned on the lights, before handing her back the keys. "The question of matrimony is still on the table. I will wait for your answer. Dream of me."

"That goes without saying. Good night, Klaus."

"Go on in," he urged quietly. "Otherwise, I will kiss you again."

"That's supposed to be a disincentive?" she challenged.

"Unless you want me to carry you up the stairs and to lay you down on your own bed, strip both of us of all our clothes, and make love with you until dawn, you had better put that door between us, now. My self-control is not quite as firm as I would like it to be where you are concerned. And I can think of nothing I would like more than to be naked with you in your bed, unless it would be to be naked with you in my bed."

"You can't stay with me until dawn. I have entirely too many windows, Klaus, for it to be safe for you to ever be present in my apartment at dawn. Goodnight," she told him, her face crimson, stepping backwards over the threshold to the shop.

Chapter Four

The air of sudden, menacing, stillness that surrounded him was remarkable. "What did you say?" he demanded in a soft, but firm, voice as he followed her into the shop and closed the door firmly behind them.

He walked over to her and stood toe to toe with her.

'Formidable' was one word that was accurate for the man standing before her. 'Intimidating' was another good word. Yet she wasn't going to back down. This was too important.

"If you project that attitude, Klaus, I'll be forced to put on my ice maiden persona. Neither of us would enjoy that," she warned quietly. "So, change the attitude, right now. You aren't impressing me, intimidating me, or frightening me."

She watched him with interest, as the threatening persona seemed to melt away, leaving only the charming man whom she had begun to come to know.

"This conversation is not going to be short," he said as he removed his overcoat and put the garment down on the counter.

Out of well-honed habits of neatness, she picked up his coat and hung it on the coat rack. Then she removed her own coat and hung it beside his.

"Just tell me why you made that comment about the windows," Klaus said softly as she turned to face him once more.

"Do you actually believe I would recklessly endanger someone for whom I cared?"

"No, recklessness is one quality no one would ever attribute to you, " he said quietly. "Suppose you tell me what you believe you know of my condition?"

"Do you think that I lack eyes, Klaus? It is true that I am not trained in medicine. However, I am a trained observer who is said to possess a good mind."

His eyes narrowed as he looked at her. "Figured it out all by yourself, did you?" he offered harshly.

"I don't have the patience tonight to deal with your defensive posturing. So, change the attitude or leave. It is entirely your choice. The door is just behind you."

"No, I am not leaving. Let us deal with this issue of caring."

"Let's not."

He smiled broadly. "Are you going to invite me upstairs, Edwina?"

"No, Klaus. I don't think it's wise at the moment."

"Suppose I promise you that when I leave you will still be a virgin?"

"Haven't we already discussed hypothetical questions?" she asked quietly.

"Invite me upstairs, Edwina. I'll behave."

"Well or badly?"

He smiled at her. "However you want me to. Tell me that you don't want me and I'll leave."

She looked at him for a long time without saying anything. "You know that I can't honestly do that. I won't lie to you."

He smiled. "I want to make love with you, tonight."

"No, Klaus, goodnight. Please leave now, before I do something I ought to regret, but probably won't."

Instead of leaving, he took her into his arms. Then he picked her up and carried her towards the stairs. "Nothing more than you allow will happen tonight between us. But we both need something more than a simple goodnight kiss."

He took the stairs with ease two at a time.

"You're not even breaking a sweat."

"You don't weigh anything."

"Yes, I do."

"I could carry you around all day."

"Obviously."

When he got upstairs with her still cradled in his arms, he walked across her living area and over to the window seat. He sat down bringing her into his lap. He continued to hold her firmly within his arms.

"This is silly," she told him. His arousal was obvious. It was all she could do not to reach down to stroke him. But the civilized part of her knew that would be wrong, since it would be starting something she didn't know if she could afford to finish.

"It is silly indeed. I'd far rather be in bed with you than cuddled together on this window seat."

"That's moving too fast for me," she told him reluctantly.

"Tell me that you wouldn't rather be here in my arms than here alone?"

"I'm never alone."

"There is someone with here you?" he demanded, his voice harsh.

"My cats."

"Cats," he replied in an echo. "How many cats do you have, Edwina?" he asked indulgently.

"Just the two. Heather and Phlox. They normally sleep in my bed."

"Lucky cats!"

"Not really. I snore."

"Do you? How do you know?"

"My cousins and dorm-mates have told me so."

He laughed in real amusement. "Only you would name your cats for flora," he said changing the subject.

"They are as good of names as any."

"Edwina, you would perhaps rather have only your cats for company? Is that what you are trying to tell me?"

"I don't lie, Klaus," she replied softly. "Well, not usually," she added wryly.

"Not even a 'white' lie, Edwina?"

"Honesty doesn't have to be brutal. But, the truth should never be avoided."

"What is the truth between us, my sweet?"

"I care about you. Probably more than I should given how short of a time we have known one another. That's all I'm willing to admit at the moment."

"It's a start, my darling," he said. "That makes me quite happy to hear. When will you marry me?"

"Don't push me, Klaus."

"You are frightened."

"Yes."

"Maybe you should be," he offered lowly.

"Maybe. You are a powerful man, physically and economically. But I believe that you have learned to be careful as well," she agreed. "I don't believe that you would ever purposefully harm anyone smaller and weaker than yourself."

He smiled at her. "You are beginning to know me and to trust me."

"Perhaps I am, at that."

"I won't promise not to rush you, Edwina. I want you desperately."

"Thanks for the warning," she teased. "I had figured that out. The ridge of your erection poking me in the hip tells me that."

"Does it? Good."

"Why is it good?"

"I have recognized the inevitability of our being together, my dear. I try not to delay the inevitable."

"But, then, if something is inevitable, why rush it? Why not simply enjoy the journey? Of all the things that are truly inevitable, death heads the list. I plan on doing everything in my power to delay that particular inevitability."

"You are in no hurry to meet St. Peter," he offered quietly.

"I'd like to put that particular meeting off as long as humanly possible."

He sighed. "There would be costs to being immortal. Costs that might be difficult to pay."

"No one wants to die."

"And no one really wants to live forever. People—like flowers—are meant to bloom only for a time, some longer than others, but a limited time for everyone."

"I still plan on putting off meeting St. Peter for as long as possible."

"As long as you do not plan on putting me off as long as possible."

"No. I believe that you fall into an entirely different category."

He laughed. "Good." Then he began to pluck the pins from her hair. "Have I told you how much I've fantasized about seeing you naked with this hair streaming down over your bare breasts."

She felt the heat rise to her face again and knew that she was blushing boldly.

"Come and dance with me," she said quietly as her hair flowed down. She rose to her feet. Dancing had to be less risky than sitting in the window seat with him.

"There is no music."

She picked up a remote and pressed one button. Guitar music filled the air. It was music meant for romance. "Now there is music."

He smiled and stood. He took her into his arms and began dancing slowly with her. "I don't recognize the piece or the artist."

"No reason you should recognize the recording. I've never shared it with anyone. It's just too evocative. I play it sometimes for myself."

"And what do you do to that music all by yourself?"

"Dream."

"Dream of what?"

"A man who will love me for who am I, and in spite of who I am will still love me," Edwina replied quietly.

Klaus kissed her forehead. "There is no need to dream. I am here."

"I can see that."

"I'm honored to hear your music."

She smiled at him. "That was the idea." Then she took his face in her hands and kissed him gently. Or at least, she intended the kiss to be gentle. But there was just too much need on both their parts for the kiss to remain soft for long.

He returned the kiss with equal hunger as he unfastened the row of tiny pearl buttons on the back of her blouse.

She pulled away from him as she felt the touch of his hand on the bare skin of her back above her camisole. "No," she said with a smile as she removed her blouse. "Last night, you gave me pleasure, tonight is for you. I don't exactly know what I'm doing, Klaus. But you'll find I'm a quick study. And we have time tonight to play a bit."

"Play?"

"Any objections?"

"How can I when I set the conditions of your remaining a virgin?" he asked dryly.

She smiled at him. "You can't."

"I'm all yours."

"Are you? Good. If you are all mine, then it's up to me what I do with you, isn't it?" she asked as she pushed the suit coat away from his shoulders. She ran her hands down his arms until the coat hit the floor.

"Yes. What do you have in mind?"

"Ah, that would be telling. Just relax and enjoy the ride, Klaus. Just don't touch me unless I ask you to. I'm not exactly in control."

"One can have too tight of a control on oneself."

"Or too little." Then she removed his tie clasp. She looked at it. "That's a nice diamond," she said quietly.

"It's yours if you want it. I could easily have it reset into an engagement ring for you."

"Diamonds are beautiful, but I'm not partial to them," she said as she placed it in the pocket of his pants.

"What kind of stone do you like?"

"I've always liked sapphires and emeralds."

"There are some good sapphires and emeralds among the family jewels."

Edwina laughed as her hand lingered in his pants pocket. "Oh, Klaus. In American slang, the 'family jewels' refer to something completely different."

"What?"

"This," she said quietly as she moved her hand to gently cup his testicles through the double fabric of the pocket and his boxers. "These are the family jewels, Klaus. No woman in her right mind would want to lose them."

"How in the world did you remain a virgin this long with your being this bold?" he asked hoarsely.

"I'm only bold with you," she told him, releasing him.

"That's good, because I'd murder any man with whom I discovered you in an intimate embrace. And then

I'd take you to bed and keep you there until you couldn't think of loving anyone but me."

She smiled at him as she untied the Windsor knot in which he had tied the silk of his tie. "There's no danger of that situation arising. I'm the faithful type."

"You are the type to drive a man to distraction."

Edwina smiled again. "Good. Then you know how I feel around you." Then she added as she began to unfasten the gold studs on his shirt. "I rather like these shirts of yours."

"Why?"

"It's like unwrapping a gift one has waited for all of one's life. It should be done slowly, deliberately, and with full enjoyment. When the wrappings are so pretty, it would be a shame to rush through them," she said just before she slid her hand between the fine linen of his shirt and the furry pelt of his chest.

Klaus made an inarticulate groan of pleasure as her fingers retreated quickly and resumed unfastening the studs on his shirt. "Woman!"

"Klaus?"

"You're driving me mad."

"I have barely begun."

"You are wicked," he said with affection in his voice.

"Am I?" she asked as she unfastened the last of his shirt studs she could see and pulled the shirt from the inside of his trousers.

"Completely."

"Then I'm succeeding," she answered as she finished the studs and began working on his cuff links. "It's rather amusing to be wicked."

"You know that turn about is fair play," he offered quietly.

"That, Klaus, is the point of this particular exercise." She peeled off his shirt and let the linen garment hit the floor with his suit coat.

The only sexier sight she had ever seen had been his completely naked body, but that had been only in her dreams.

"Michelangelo could have sculpted you," she said quietly, almost reverently as she touched his chest. "You have a beautiful form, Klaus."

Edwina dropped a kiss at the juncture of his neck and shoulder.

"I'm glad that you think so," he said hoarsely.

She looked at him and smiled as she stroked his face. "No false modesty, Klaus. You are all too aware of how attractive you are and of how deeply women ache to touch you."

"Do you ache to touch me?"

"Only when I'm not touching you. When I'm touching you, there is a decidedly different sort of ache."

"I can ease that ache," he offered as he cupped her breasts through the cotton of her camisole. His thumbs lightly rubbed her hard nipples.

She drew a deep breath then she smiled at him. "Did I ask you to touch me?"

"No."

"Then hands off."

"Yes, m'am," he said as he dropped his hands to his sides.

Edwina giggled as she dropped to her knees and began to loosen his shoes. One foot at a time, she removed his shoes and socks. "Klaus, what am I to do with you?"

"I could make some pertinent suggestions," he offered as she rose to her feet once more.

She giggled again as she unfastened her skirt's waistband and let the garment drop to the floor. She stepped out of the circle of fabric. "I'll just bet you could," she said as she stood before him in her white cotton floor length slip and camisole.

"You are so beautiful, Edwina Elizabeth."

She shook her head in denial. "I'm glad you think so. Now, come with me."

He followed her into her bathroom, leaving the door open behind him. As bathrooms went, this one was more than merely functional, and less than truly sybaritic. There was a separate garden tub and a shower. There were green plants all around the room, green plants and some of the most beautiful rare orchids that he had ever seen. The delicate scent of the orchids was enticing. There were also two cats—both seal point Siamese—curled up on the marble ledge of the tub. The cats opened their eyes and stretched before standing and jumping down from the ledge. The cats *meyouwed* and left the room.

She started the water running in the tub. The water pressure was strong and the tub was beginning to fill quite quickly. "I'll be back in a few minutes. Stay here. Shut the tap off when the water is about a half of an inch over the jets, any more than that and it will overflow when we both get in."

Klaus looked at her departing back and smiled. What was she up to? The idea of having her in his arms naked with the water massaging them without possessing her was almost more than he could bear. This woman was a temptress, or at least a temptress in training. He could hardly wait until she became surer of herself.

It was a pretty room. It suited her. She had pillar candles set all around the room. Those candles had obviously been burned before. He could imagine her in this room, the lights off, the candles burning providing soft light, and her naked form in the tub soaking away the tension of the day.

When she returned to the bathroom, she was wearing a green tankini-style swimsuit and had piled her hair on the top of her head in a loose knot. In her hand was a man's extremely brief swimsuit with a well-known brand emblem printed on the right front. It took little imagination to know that suit was new as the price tag was still attached. In her other arm, she was carrying a silver wine cooler with a bottle in it. Two tulip glasses were in her hand.

She looked at the tub. It was just about full enough. She put down the glasses and the wine on the ledge around the tub. Then, she snapped off the plastic string holding the price tag onto the swimsuit. "I'd bought this for a cousin as a joke going-away present. He's spending a year in Antarctica at a research station. But at the last moment, I decided not to give it to him. He would have found some way of sending me a photo with him wearing it outdoors in a snow drift, even if he had to manipulate a couple of digital photos to do that. I would have never lived it down." She realized that she was rambling. "The suit should fit you."

Then she turned off the flow of water into the tub and turned on the jets.

Klaus smiled at her. "You are full of surprises."

"Am I?" she dismissed as she stepped around him and began to light the candles around the room. "Do you like candles?"

Klaus followed her around the room. He placed a hand on her shoulder. "You don't have to be this nervous."

She looked up into the mirror and spoke to his reflection. "Do you want something to drink?" she asked him. "It's a very nice bottle of white wine."

"Edwina, do you want me to leave?" he asked hesitantly.

She bit her lower lip. "No. Come and sit in the tub and relax with me. I've had fantasies about relaxing in that tub with you." She didn't tell him that she had those particular fantasies since before she had seen the tub at the plumbing supply house. And that she had redrawn all of the plans for the rooms in this apartment to accommodate the tub. It was a luxury item and had taken quite a chunk of money she could have put to better use. Yet, tonight, she believed it to be worth every cent she had spent.

"Face me, *Liebling*," he said gently.

She turned to face him.

"You are trembling."

There was no sense in denying it. "Yes."

He murmured a string of endearments in rapid German as she came into his arms.

"I have to be insane," she said quietly. "I can't think of anything that I want more than to be with you and I'm putting obstacles in our way."

"There is no hurry. Time is not of the essence in this relationship."

"I was planning on taking off your pants and pulling on those tight little trunks that leave so little to the imagination."

Klaus laughed. "Like that swimsuit of yours?"

"Something like that."

"The water will cool."

"There's an in-line heater. It will stay hot for a long time."

"Good. Like I said earlier, I'm all yours. Do as you wish."

Her fingers closed around his belt buckle. "I'm a coward, Klaus."

"Hardly."

She smiled at him as she unfastened his belt, then the zipper and hook on his trousers. The garment puddled on the floor at his feet, leaving him standing there with only his boxers on.

Edwina's mouth went dry. Gathering her courage, she pushed that remnant of his clothing from him as well. Smiling, he stepped backwards out of the clothing that lay at his feet.

"Edwina?" he asked carefully.

"I stand by my earlier assessment. It is a shame we cannot transport Michelangelo through time to sculpt you in marble, life sized. You are a beautiful man."

Klaus stepped over his clothes and came to her. "Marble is terribly cold to the touch."

"And you are anything except cold."

He smiled at her. "Now that you've gotten me out of my clothes, what are you going to do with me?"

"Anything I want to. For now come and soak. We could use a little play time."

"Yes. But, by whose rules are we playing?"

"Mine."

"Could I know what they are?"

"How can you when I don't? I'm making this up as I go along."

Klaus laughed. "Very well, Edwina. Shall I put on the suit?"

"You seem comfortable in your skin."

"Are you not?"

She looked down at the swimsuit she wore. "Obviously not."

Klaus climbed into the tub. Edwina followed him into the water. She sat beside him. His arm went around her shoulder. She rested her head on his shoulder, enjoying the comfort of his embrace.

"This is the best moment of my day," Klaus told her.

She looked at him and smiled. "Oh, I think it will get better."

"What do you have in mind?"

"Just relax, Klaus. You'll be home far before dawn."

"I appreciate that."

She reached over and poured two glasses of the wine. Then she handed him one of those.

"Dutch courage?" he asked.

"No. I just like this wine. I thought you might enjoy a glass or two of it as well."

He took the glass from her and sipped. "You have good taste. This is very fine."

"You are very fine," she told him after she drank from her own glass and then put it down.

Klaus took another sip of his wine and set the glass down on the ledge of the tub. "Edwina, when will you marry me?"

"Why would you want to commit to me?"

He looked at her as though she had just asked a profoundly stupid question. "That should be obvious. I'm in love with you."

"You fall in love this easily?"

"No. I've felt this way about only one other woman in my whole life."

"Why didn't you marry her?"

"She's dead. She died many years ago."

"I'm sorry, Klaus," Edwina said quietly, touching his face, then kissing him softly.

She had intended the kiss to be brief, nothing more than a brush of her lips against his. But her body had other ideas. So much for relaxation.

Edwina found herself moving to straddle Klaus' legs as the kiss deepened between them.

"This was a bad idea," she said quietly as she looked at his face.

"Feels like a very good idea to me. The only better idea would be if you would take off that bathing suit."

"I'm not quite as comfortable in my skin as you are in yours."

"Being somewhat clothed makes you feel more in control."

She nodded slightly.

"You have control issues."

"Many people do, I hear," she said just before she reached down, grasped the hem of the swimsuit top and pulled it off over her head. "But I can compromise."

Klaus' hands came up to cup her breasts. "You are so beautiful. Your breasts are lovely. I envy our children taking nourishment."

"There is no reason to envy them, Klaus."

He smiled at her before he brought his mouth to her right breast.

Need shot through her as he began to alternately lave and suck her nipple. His fingers lightly rolled her other nipple.

She threw her head back and arched against him, offering him more of her breasts.

It was an offer he wasn't in the least shy about taking.

Klaus' hands went to her hips and gently urged her to settle down into contact with his penis. Even through the double fabric of her bikini bottom, the sensation of having his glans pressed against her clitoris took her breath away.

"Thought that I asked you not to touch me," she offered quietly.

"I couldn't help myself."

"Good. I can't help myself, either."

"Edwina, we'll play if you want. It's all I can do not to rip that bikini off you, then ram into you. All I want is to be inside you. I want to hear you moan and know that the sound is pleasure. I want to see you orgasm. I want to feel you orgasm around me, time and time again. I could feel that forever and never tire of it."

She swallowed hard as she saw the seriousness in his eyes and felt him tremble as she touched his chest.

Edwina rose to her feet and climbed out of the tub. She picked up a large towel and wrapped it around herself as a sarong. Then, she picked up another and held it out to him. "Let me dry you."

He rose and came to her.

Her mouth went dry once more as she looked at his lean but powerful body. She tried not to look at his erect penis. However, she could hardly ignore it.

She went to work removing the water from him. Edwina walked behind him and dried the water from his back. She went down on her knees and dried his butt and the backs of his legs. Before she rose to her feet, she planted a light kiss on the birthmark on his butt. It was a mark that she had seen many times in her dreams.

Through the light contact of her lips to his birthmark, Edwina felt him shudder. And she smiled. His control was perilous. She knew that she was playing with fire. She knew from her dreams just how hot that fire could burn.

"*Frau!*" he moaned. Then he demanded hoarsely in German, "How long are you planning to torture me like this?"

"You set the conditions for your coming upstairs, Klaus," she said as she rose to her feet and came around to dry his front. "And you are a beautiful man. I think that we have a long ways to go yet in becoming fully comfortable with one another," she said as she moved the towel slowly down his chest and flat stomach.

"You are enjoying this," he accused.

"Of course I am. That was the point of the exercise. You are enjoying it, too."

"I can think of things we would both enjoy more."

Edwina dropped to her knees again and began to dry his legs. She allowed her right cheek to brush his penis. And she smiled as she heard him moan. Then she moved to dry his other leg. Her left cheek brushed his penis.

When his legs were dry, she took the towel and lightly, but firmly, dried his penis and scrotum.

Remembering his reaction from a dream, she gathered her courage. She took the tip of his penis into her mouth and ran her tongue around the glans. Then she backed away from him before she began to drop light kisses along the length of his penis and then on his scrotum.

"Don't stop," Klaus begged in German.

"You like this?"

"*Frau!*" he said affection in his voice. "You know I like it."

"Just making sure," she replied before she took his penis back into her mouth and began to move her head rhythmically up and down his erect shaft. Klaus' hands threaded through her hair. Edwina felt her hair loosen and stream down her back.

Edwina wrapped her arms around him and began to knead his buttocks with her hands. She heard him moan with excitement once more. She focused on giving him pleasure. His pleasure was exciting her.

Realizing that he was about ready to ejaculate, she debated about taking the semen in her mouth or pulling away. He was so sexually experienced that she simply wanted to slap him when she thought about the number of women he had likely been with during his life.

Reluctantly, she pulled away from him and replaced her mouth with her hand. As he began to climax, she grabbed the towel from the floor and caught his semen in it. Then she threw the towel into the clothes hamper after he finished.

She rose to her feet and picked up her glass of wine. She took a drink before she looked at him.

"Turn about is fair play, Edwina," he said quietly as he pulled her into his arms.

She smiled at him then brushed a kiss along his cheek. Then she stepped back from him. "Put your trousers back on, Klaus. Take the wine into my library. We can sit there for a little while. I need to have a minute to myself, right now."

Klaus smiled at her, then picked up his trousers. With a few swift motions, he had boxers and trousers back on his body.

"You are so incredibly sexy," she told him.

He chuckled. "*Frau*," he said in rapid German, "you are the one in this room who is sexy. I can hardly keep my hands off you. There will never be a time that I will fail to desire you."

"Even if I put on hundreds of pounds of weight and go gray?" she teased.

He pulled the towel loose from her and looked at her nearly bare body. "All I would have to do is to remember how you look right now. You are so beautiful to me. The memory of this moment will stay with me for a very long time."

"Go on. Give me a minute or two."

"Very well."

"The log in the fireplace is gas. All you do is have to turn it on. It is self-lighting. I feel like a sitting before a fire with you."

"You are a fire."

"Am I? Good. Now go, please."

"Very well, Edwina."

When the door closed behind him, she peeled off the bikini bottom and finished drying herself. She refreshed her perfume. Then Edwina walked over to the closet and pulled out a black and silver silk caftan along with the matching slippers that her cousin Marie had presented her with as a Christmas gift. She had no sooner gotten that on over her head when the cats howled and the temperature in the room dropped precipitously.

"Go away, Catherine," Edwina said firmly without turning around to face the spirit. She left the bathroom without paying the spirit any more attention.

Walking into the library, she saw that Klaus had lit the fire. He had put on his shirt, but the sleeves were rolled up. He was reading the titles from her bookshelves. "You have quite eclectic taste in literature, Edwina Elizabeth," he said without turning to face her.

"That's putting it mildly," she said as she crossed the room to stand beside him.

Klaus had put on his shirt, but it was still unfastened. He'd also put back on his shoes. Without thinking, she reached out and touched his chest.

"You do like playing with fire, don't you, Edwina?" he asked in amusement

"That has become painfully obvious."

"Why painfully?"

"Klaus, you are sweeping me off my feet. I hardly know what I'm about anymore."

"Do you want me to go away?" he asked carefully.

"No, not at all. But it is getting late."

"You have quite a selection of books on the supernatural. They are old books."

"Those were my father's. The occult held a fascination for him. He particularly was fascinated by the impact of myth and legend upon culture."

"Have you read these works?"

"Most of them, at one time or another."

"And what do you think about the impact of…say…vampire legends upon culture?"

She shrugged. "There is certainly a preponderance of those legends in every culture around the globe. No two regional legends are quite the same. However, those legends have definitely become part of the popular culture. There is a certain canon of vampire lore that is common at least in the States. Just do a search on the Internet for the word 'vampire' if you doubt that. Browse the horror or even the romance shelves at a bookstore or walk through a video rental store and look for the number of titles directly or indirectly related to vampiric legends. There is a substantial body of work in print and in one video format or another. Walk through a discount store in the month before Halloween. You'll see all manner of vampire symbols, costumes, accessories."

"But, what do you think about the impact of the legends upon culture? You've described some of the impact."

A shrill alarm sounded before she could reply.

"*Fire!*" Edwina announced needlessly as she walked over to the monitor and checked the location of the fire. It was in the paint store, the store owned by the tenant who had been quite loud in his protests about poltergeists. Klaus had turned off the gas log and was standing beside her.

"Time to get out of here?"

"Yes."

Edwina checked the door at the head of the stairs for heat, finding none, she opened it and headed down the stairs. The alarm was still sounding. Reaching the shop, she felt around the door for heat, and finding none, went into the shop. There was no sign of fire. She snatched up her building keys and tossed Klaus his coat before putting on her own as she grabbed two fire extinguishers from under the counter. They left the shop and ran down three shops to the paint store

In the paint store, she saw the glow of a small fire coming from the back of the store.

The sirens of the fire department truck were approaching.

She unlocked the door to the paint store.

Klaus followed her into the shop and back to the area from where the smoke and flames seemed to come. The smoke wasn't too bad, yet. He took the fire extinguisher from her and aimed it at the trash-can from where the flames were still mostly contained, although they had begun to creep up a wall. It didn't take long to put out the fire, but it did take both extinguishers.

Edwina went over to her tenant who was lying on the floor, unconscious, in a small pool of his own blood. She checked for a pulse. He had one, although it was weak and thready. It was clear that someone had attacked him then set a fire. The back door to the shop was partially open as if someone had fled that way and hadn't taken the time to shut the door firmly behind him.

She looked over at Klaus. "This is a mess."

"We'll get through it. Is he alive?"

"For now. I don't want to move him. The fire out?"

"Seems to be. You want me to check him over?"

She sighed heavily. "There are advantages of having a doctor in the house."

"There are many advantages to keeping me around, Edwina," Klaus replied carefully.

"I had discovered that."

The firemen came through the door before Klaus could examine Jim.

"We put the fire out," Klaus told them. "But we need an ambulance for him."

The first fireman in the door nodded. "Come on out of the shop. We'll take care of this."

It was two a.m. before Edwina and Klaus were done with giving statements to the police and fire department. Jim Douglass, her tenant, had come to alertness and had been taken to the hospital for treatment of his injuries. The fire department pronounced the fire to be out.

The reason for the failure of the fire sprinkler system was found. Someone had encased every sprinkler head the shop inside lumps of a thick, quick setting, clear acrylic resin, clogging the heads so effectively that water could not flow out. This was looking less and less like a robbery with every passing moment. Everyone seemed certain that someone had wanted Jim dead and wanted to destroy the evidence by burning down the building.

Edwina put in a call to the company that had installed the system, leaving a message that there was urgent service needed on the sprinkler system. The sprinkler heads would have to be replaced as soon as possible. She told them that she was willing to pay extra for a Sunday service call.

Klaus walked her back to her shop door.

"Goodnight, Klaus," she said as they stopped before her shop door.

"Are you certain that you want to go back upstairs? The odor of smoke is bound to waft up there."

"I'll open some windows if it becomes unbearable. It was a minor fire, Klaus. I don't think there's really any problem."

He sighed. "I guess that means that you are not going to invite me back upstairs?"

"No. I'm not. Not tonight. It's very late." She leaned into him and lightly kissed him on the lips. "Goodnight."

"Sleep well, Edwina."

"Drive safely."

"Dream of me."

"I don't think I have any choice in the matter," she said dryly.

Klaus looked at her curiously, but all he said was 'goodnight' before he walked away.

Catherine blinked in when Edwina returned to her apartment.

"You know, von Bruner wants to marry you," Catherine said.

"That would be his problem."

"No, my dear, I rather believe that it is your problem. Don't dream of him. It's dangerous. He's dangerous. Marriage to him would be the last mistake you would ever make," and with that, the shade faded out.

Chapter Five

Edwina paced, her bare feet sinking into the pile of a luxuriously thick red carpet. She wore an off-white silk and lace negligee. She was torn between staying here with him and running. She didn't know what frightened her most about the prospect of running, the strong probability that he would come after her, or the remote possibility that he wouldn't. This was her choice. He'd said that. She knew he wouldn't force anything upon her.

Then she looked around the room. A fire crackled in a great stone fireplace. An open bottle of wonderful champagne was iced in an antique silver cooler. That sat on a silver tray on the bedside table along with two half-empty pieces of crystal stemware.

A Chopin piano concerto was playing softly in the background. The only other sounds in the room were the crackling of the fire and her breathing.

She poured herself another glass of champagne. She admired the way that the firelight bounced off the large marquis cut grass green emerald of her engagement ring. The stone had a tremendous amount of fire. When he had given her the ring he had said that the fire of the stone was secondary to the fire of her eyes. She didn't know if that was true. The stone was incredibly beautiful. And so was the narrow wedding band of platinum and diamonds that she wore with the engagement ring.

Then she walked over to the security monitor in the windowless room and looked out at the midnight storm. The rain was coming down in sheets. Flashes of lightning lit up the partially planted garden. She picked up the planting diagrams for the garden and noticed that they were in her handwriting. The new garden was going to be so beautiful.

Of course, with this amount of rain, she thought, it was going to take a week or so before it would be dry enough for the crew to get back in to finish the work. But by the Fourth of July, it would be a beautiful setting for the midnight fireworks party Klaus was planning.

Klaus entered the bedroom from the attached bathroom. At the sound of the door opening, she turned to look at him.

He wore only a silk brocade dressing gown. "I wasn't certain that you would still be here," he said from the doorway.

"I wasn't either," she admitted quietly.

Klaus crossed the room to her. "I'm glad you stayed. Have you made a decision, Edwina?"

She drank from her glass of champagne.

He took the glass from her hand and drained the last quarter of the glass from the same place that she had drunk. Then he put the glass down on the bed table. "We don't need intoxicants, you and I. Or are you screwing up your courage?"

She smiled at him. "No, we don't need intoxicants. You're quite intoxicating enough. And I don't need to screw up my courage. There's nothing to be courageous about. I've made my decision. I want all the time with you that I can have, regardless of the costs."

He laughed. "You are so beautiful." He removed the hairpins, dropping them one by one onto the floor. Then he raked his fingers through her hair. "I've dreamed of seeing you like this, Edwina, in the firelight, with your hair down, dressed in silk and lace, in this room, loving me."

She reached out and slipped her hand between the fabric and his chest, touching him lightly. "I'm not a dream. I'm real. Don't I feel real to you?"

He shuddered under her touch. "Edwina, if you were any more real, I don't think I could stand it."

She laughed softly. "And, just for the record I do love you, more than I ever thought I could love anyone. If I didn't, I wouldn't have stood before the priest and made those vows to you and I wouldn't be here now. I love you so much it scares me."

"You aren't the only one who is scared, sweetheart." He pulled her into his arms. Her fingers laced through his hair as his mouth covered hers. She returned his passion with her own. She was on fire for him. Behind her closed eyes, colors swirled wildly. She was hot, then cold, then hot again. Overwhelming desire became simple necessity, much as it always had between them.

Her trembling fingers moved towards the robe belt. She untied it and pushed the heavy robe away from his shoulders, down his arms, until it was a puddle of cloth around his feet. He wore nothing else under the robe.

Klaus lifted his mouth from hers. He spoke in German, his voice thick with passion. "This is your last chance to walk away from me. If you give yourself to me as I wish you to tonight, I will keep you. I keep and care for what is mine. This is forever. I need you to be certain that you want to be mine forever, Edwina. Once the transition is made, there is no undoing it."

She pressed her silk covered body against his naked form. "I know what I want, Klaus. And an eternity isn't nearly long enough to love you."

Klaus pushed the negligee from her shoulders. It joined his dressing gown on the floor.

She took him by the hand and walked to his large canopied bed. He pulled the quilted bed-curtains closed behind them. Inside, it was completely dark. The silk sheets were smooth and light against her skin.

"I can't see you, Klaus," she complained.

"Don't see. Close your eyes. Keep them closed. Just feel, sweetheart," he advised softly as he caressed her breasts. "I need you to want me. The transition will be less painful if you are aroused fully and lost in pleasure."

"I am!"

But he wasn't satisfied with that. He set about to arouse her even more through the use of his hands and mouth. Nothing mattered to her except his erotic touches and the ministrations of his mouth on her breasts, on her belly, on her thighs, in the soft, hot, folds of her labia.

She heard her own voice moan his name, "Klaus. Klaus. Please, I need…"

And she heard him answer hoarsely, "Not until you want me the way I want you. I don't want to ever hurt you, Edwina."

His touches and kisses were incendiary. Each nerve in her body felt as though it was on sensory overload. She wanted to scream with the utter pleasure he was giving her. And then suddenly she did call out his name as the tension he had been building in her released. In spite of that, he continued arousing her, building on the climax, urging her towards another even more shattering release.

The sound of the phone ringing snapped her into wakefulness. Yet the dream lingered. Or was it merely a dream? It was too real to have been a simple dream. But this particular type of dream was always too real.

The phone was insistent. She moved and her head let her know that she'd overindulged in wine the night before. The clock said eight fifteen a.m..

She gingerly picked up the receiver and put it to her ear. On the other end was her grandmother. "Good morning, Edwina Elizabeth."

"Good morning, Grandmother," she said with a yawn as she tried to clear the dream away from her mind. Yet the images lingered.

"You sound sleepy, child. Did I wake you?"

"Yes."

"Oh, I am sorry, my dear child! You are normally up long before now."

"I was out quite late last night."

"Out with some handsome gentleman?" the old woman asked hopefully.

"As a matter of fact, I was."

"That is good news! When am I to meet this gentleman friend of yours?"

"I don't know, Grandmother."

"I see," her grandmother replied in a disapproving voice. "Edwina, you are past the age when you can afford to engage in relationships which fail to have marriage as their primary goal. You are far too old to be taking casual lovers."

Edwina closed her eyes and sighed. "Thank you. I am well aware of my advanced age. For your information, I am not in the habit of taking lovers, casual or otherwise. If I were in such a habit, I certainly would not have spent the night in a lonely bed. The gentleman would have been more than willing to stay if I had permitted such a thing. But I sent him home."

"There is no need to use that tone with me, young woman!" her grandmother warned quietly.

Edwina laughed. "One moment, you are telling me that I'm getting old, and the next you're calling me young. I really just can't win with you, can I, Grandmother?"

"Tell me about this man you are seeing."

"I don't think so, Grandmother. It's too new. Let me figure him out before I subject him to the scrutiny of the family."

"You are more than slightly fond of him? I hear it in your voice."

"Perhaps. I think I will probably marry him."

Edwina could hear the smile in her grandmother's voice. "You bring him around to meet me. Luncheon today, after Mass. I want to meet this man who has gotten beyond my granddaughter's formidable defenses."

"I can make no promises, Grandmother. Klaus and I had made no plans for today. He has an extra full schedule for today. I don't expect to see him. We do not live in one another's pockets."

"Klaus? He's German? What's his last name?"

"Von Bruner."

"One of my great-grandmother's sisters married into the von Bruner family from Bavaria. It's a good Catholic family, a family of minor nobility — a Baron I believe. This man, Klaus, he isn't divorced is he?"

"He's a bachelor."

"How old?"

"Forty-one."

"That's a good age for a man to marry. At least, he's dry behind the ears and you would be his mid-life crisis. All in all, that's a pretty good combination."

Edwina laughed. "You do have original ways of thinking about things."

"Be here and bring him. I want to see this man," the old lady commanded. Then she said, "Goodbye, Edwina. I expect you and your gentleman for luncheon."

The next sound she heard was the click of the receiver.

Catherine, the shade, faded in. "I'm surprised at you, Edwina. That was quite a dream. Don't trust him. Klaus von Bruner will destroy you. He'll use and discard you, the same way that he has all the other women in his life. And there have been many women in his life, for a long, long, time. He steals their souls from them then either leaves them or drives them to suicide. There are rumors whispered that he actually murdered a couple of women while in passion. But no one has been able to turn up the bodies."

"Oh, go away, Catherine," Edwina snapped wearily.

"Remember my warning. I'm going way out of my way here to be nice to you about this." Then the shade began to fade away. "I don't even want to think about the number of rules that I'm breaking by giving you a warning about the creature."

Edwina picked up her dream journal and quickly recorded the dream. She drew a quick ink sketch of the room from two different perspectives. Only after she did this, was she ready to call Klaus with the lunch invitation.

She wasn't at all certain that she wanted to talk to Klaus, not given the intensity of the dream she had just had about him. But knowing that inviting Klaus was a direct order from her grandmother and if she didn't invite him her grandmother would, Edwina dialed Klaus's phone number.

A very formal sounding male voice answered the phone.

"Edwina Johnson calling for *Herr* von Bruner."

"One moment, please, *Fraulein* Doctor Johnson. I shall transfer the call immediately," the man replied then he put her on hold.

"Edwina," Klaus said gently. "Good morning. You are calling early."

"My grandmother just called. She wishes to meet you. We've been invited there for luncheon."

"I take it this is rather a command performance?" he asked dryly.

Edwina sighed. "Something of that nature. Trust me, my grandmother is the original formidable lady."

"Then she is something like her granddaughter. I sincerely regret that I am unable to comply with the request."

"I told Grandmother that you would not be able to attend. You aren't obligated in the least, Klaus," Edwina said gently. "I really just wanted to hear your voice this morning."

"I'm honored that your grandmother has invited me. The fact that I've been invited says that you are taking my proposal seriously enough to talk with her about it. I only regret that I am unable to fulfill the obligation."

"I need to get ready for Church," Edwina said, changing the subject. "Mass is in two hours."

"You know, you always do that."

"Do what?"

"Change the subject whenever it grows uncomfortable for you."

Edwina sighed. "Perhaps I do. However, I do need to get ready for Mass."

"Pray for me."

"Of course. Do you go to Mass regularly, Klaus?"

"The Cardinal was kind enough, because of my condition, to allow me a small chapel in my home. My chaplain says Mass for me and my household staff, daily."

"You have your own chaplain," she echoed.

"Actually, he's chaplain to the corporation and chairs our bio-ethics committee. He's a Religious, not a diocesan priest. Providing the sacraments to me is the least of the many items in his job description."

"I still can't get over the fact that you have your own chaplain."

"It is necessary. I'd be guaranteed to be able to hear Mass only twice a year—Christmas Eve and Easter Vigil otherwise."

"That makes sense," she said with a yawn.

"You are not a morning person, I take it?" he asked carefully.

"Normally, I am. But I don't normally stay up until the wee hours of the morning. Well, I'll let you go."

"Did you dream of me, Edwina?"

"I choose not to answer that on the grounds that my answer would only serve to inflate your already far too highly bloated ego."

He laughed in genuine amusement. "You wound me."

"If you were serious in that complaint, I would apologize."

"I believe that you would at that."

"Goodbye, Klaus."

"Call me anytime. Regardless of what I'm doing, I will always take time for you."

"That's a broad promise."

"It's nothing more than the truth," he protested.

"Klaus, I don't know what to make of you."

"That's a start. At least you aren't dismissing me out of hand."

"No woman in her right mind would dismiss you out of hand."

Klaus laughed. "And this description applies to you, how?" he teased in what she knew was a payback for her earlier comments.

Edwina laughed then regretted it. Her head was pounding. "How much did we drink last night?"

"Hung over?" he asked tenderly.

"Just a little headache."

"May I come by this evening?"

"I'll meet you for dinner. Name the restaurant and the time."

"I won't be free until eight. I'll meet you at your shop about nine. Then we'll go somewhere for dinner."

"Klaus, you're going to have a full day. You don't need..." she began.

"On the contrary, I do need to spend the evening with you," he said smoothly, cutting her off. "And if you're honest with yourself, you'll admit the same thing about me."

"Klaus," she began again.

"Do I confuse you, Edwina?"

"I wouldn't say 'confuse' exactly. More like baffle."

"What baffles you about me?"

"Do you have a fireplace in your bedroom?" she asked suddenly.

His answer was silence for a long moment. "Yes," he answered quietly. "Why do you ask?"

"Bedrooms say a lot about us."

"And what does your bedroom say about you?" Klaus asked, turning the question back on her. "You didn't let me in there last night."

"It's fairly monastic."

"You sleep on a pile of straw covered with a blanket?" he teased.

"Not hardly. But my bedroom furniture can charitably be called utilitarian. I've put my money into the nursery, greenhouses, the shop, and those rooms of my apartment that are likely to see guests. As long as I have a place to sleep and somewhere to work, I'm happy."

"Why did you really ask me about my bedroom?"

"I've been trying to imagine what sort of room you would choose to sleep in," she said quietly.

"So, tell me what you've imagined."

"Why not?" she asked quietly. She needed to know if the dream was just her imagination or something more. It was the prospect of something more that really frightened her. She didn't like her prophetic dreams. "You strike me as the type to have luxuriously thick carpet, probably in some high energy color like red."

He was quiet for a moment. "Very accurate. The carpet in my bedroom is being replaced next week. The new carpet is red. The current carpet is white. I hate it. Go on. What else do you imagine?"

"The fireplace would be substantial, probably with a mantle of white or gray stone with a substantial hearth in gray stone."

"It's light gray stone with a darker stone hearth."

"The furnishings are heavy, dark wood, antique. The bed probably has a canopy and bed curtains quilted and heavy enough so that when they are pulled that a person can be in bed with no knowledge of whether it is day or night."

"My bed is antique mahogany. A canopied four-poster with quilted bed-curtains. Tell me what else you've imagined," Klaus demanded.

"There are built in book cases loaded with well read volumes in several languages. Comfortable wing chairs, covered in supple russet leather, with matching ottomans. An oil painting over the mantle, a seascape in a storm. You strike me as the type who would like storms. A computer and telecommunications devices are the only modern accommodations in the room. You wouldn't be without them because you are like me in that you have flashes of insight in the night and need to put those down before you forget them. There are no windows in the room. Yet you'd have a security monitor that let you see what was going on outside as well as in other parts of the house. There's a bathroom immediately attached to the bedroom. It's sybaritic in its luxury—lots of marble, gold taps, etc—yet profoundly tasteful in its execution, like it's owner."

He was quiet for a long moment. "You have an amazingly good imagination. Or have you had me investigated?"

"Like I've had time to have you investigated, even if I had the spare money," she dismissed. "My life does not revolve around you, *Herr* Doctor von Bruner."

"It will," he said with confidence. "Just as mine already revolves around you."

"Klaus…" she said lowly, stunned at this statement from him.

"How did you know these things?" he asked, changing the subject.

"I didn't know. Like I said, it was idle imagination," she replied in a weaker voice than she wanted to use.

"Imagination, maybe, but that's not the whole story. Tell me the full truth."

She sighed. Whatever had possessed her to bring up the matter in the first place? But now that she had, it was time to see what kind of reaction this would get. "No. It's not the whole story. I had a dream."

"You dreamt about my bedroom?" he asked in disbelief.

"Not precisely."

He laughed softly. "Ah, the bedroom was a backdrop, then. The dream was about us."

"Yes."

"Was it a good dream?" he asked smoothly.

"I was awakened by the telephone before it played itself out fully."

"Was it a good dream?"

"It was profoundly sensual."

"It doesn't have to stay a dream. Anything you can dream, I can make real."

"We don't know each other well enough yet for me to make an eternal commitment to you."

He was quiet for a moment. "We will, Edwina. We will."

"We'll see, Klaus. Now, I have to get ready for Sunday Mass. Then I'll be going out to my grandmother's for lunch."

"Have a good time."

"She isn't going to be happy about my coming out there alone."

"I'm sorry, Edwina. I simply can not come to lunch with you."

"Don't be sorry. I know that you can't tolerate UV. This was really short notice. On longer notice, maybe we can arrange dinner for the family one night."

"Yes. I would love to host your family for dinner. I'm sorry that you are in a bind with your grandmother, today."

"I can handle Grandmother. Her bark is much worse than her bite. She does mean well. She's just of the school that believes that the way a woman can be happy is if she's married and has a dozen children."

"Did she have a dozen children?"

"As a matter of fact, she did."

"You like children?"

"I do."

"Then you should have several."

"I'm starting way too late to have a large family. I might manage two or three children, if I find the right man."

"You have found the only man for you, Edwina," Klaus said firmly. "Accept this, and stop wasting time. I am the only man for you."

"Time will tell about that, Klaus."

"You were an only child," he offered.

"Yes. But, I had lots of cousins, so it wasn't so bad."

"But you want children, not just one child?"

She closed her eyes and pictured the children she and Klaus would have together, at least as her dreams depicted them. "Yes. I want children. I want your children."

He drew a sharp breath. "Edwina, I hate to do this especially as this conversation is just becoming truly interesting. I have a business conference call scheduled right now with several members of my board of directors. The call is coming in right now. It's been on the schedule for three weeks. We'll have to continue this interesting discussion later."

"Then, I'll let you go. Sorry to bother you this morning."

"You're never a bother. Call me anytime."

Edwina hung up the phone and then went into her little kitchen. She brewed a small pot of very strong coffee and downed three aspirin before she took a steaming shower. That helped to relieve the headache somewhat. After she finished, she both put up her hair into the customary knot at that nape of her neck and did her make up in the usual understated style—a touch of foundation, a little lip-gloss.

Grandmother was a stickler for hats and gloves on ladies. Heaven forbid that any of the female grandchildren should ever wear slacks in Grandmother's presence.

She had gone through five changes of clothes before she settled on a navy blue silk suit, with a white silk scarf draped on the inside to simulate a shawl-collared blouse. She wore her mother's pearls. It was proper, but it was also a little on the daring side. Of course, with the hat, the matching purse and shoes, and the obligatory white gloves, she looked as though she had stepped out of a fashion magazine in the 1950s or before. With her dark blue cashmere coat, Edwina knew that she would be warm enough.

Edwina had no sooner finished dressing than the phone rang. It was Jim, her paint store tenant.

"How are you feeling?"

"I'm alive."

"How's the head?"

"Hard. I've got a little concussion from where I was hit. But it will heal. I want to talk to you about my lease."

"I don't normally do business on Sundays. Talk to me tomorrow," she said quietly.

"You and your religious quackery," he said harshly. Then he slammed the phone down sharply.

"And you have a pleasant day, too, Jim."

Twenty minutes later, as she passed the paint store, Jim Douglass, her tenant came out. "Edwina!" he called after her, his voice insistent.

"I'm on my way to Church, Jim. Can it wait?"

"No, it damn well can't wait. I've had it. These poltergeists are destroying my business. You saw what they did last night. You need to do something about this."

"If you really believe that you have evil spirits in your shop, Jim, then I suggest you find a priest and have the space blessed or exorcised. I'll underwrite the cost of the stipend and supplies," she offered quietly. "That has been my offer to you all along."

"That's so much superstitious Catholic mumbo-jumbo. It won't work. Nothing about Catholicism is true. It's all so much superstitious pap designed to keep people from the truth."

She sighed and rolled her eyes. "You are entitled to your opinion, Jim, erroneous though it may be."

"What, beside your superstitious nonsense, do you propose to do about this plague of poltergeists in my store?" he demanded harshly.

"Superstition is hardly a word I'd associate with the Holy Faith," she replied. "It is however a word I would associate with a man who truly believes he is being plagued by noisy ghosts who attacked him and set a fire."

"You are a royal bitch, you know that?" Jim said angrily.

"No, that is one thing I most definitely am not," Edwina told the tenant. "Goodbye Jim."

"Just wait a damned minute," Jim screamed as he grabbed her arm with bruising force.

Edwina cast a disdainful glare at his hand as it held her arm. "Remove that hand from me if you want to keep your hand attached to your arm," she said coldly. "You have until I count to three. One … two…"

He released her and stepped back. "I am not happy."

"That much has been painfully obvious from the first moment that I met you. What would it take to make you happy?" she asked.

"You will let me out of my lease and pay to relocate my store. Move me into one of the major malls. Pay my rent for three months and all my moving expenses."

"Why would I do that? You were here well before I bought the building. I had nothing to do with the conditions you claim are intolerable."

"You either get rid of the ghosts, or we'll all launch a rent strike. None of us are happy about this haunting situation."

"I've offered to take action to rid you of the spirits you say you have," she said quietly. "I've made you that offer in writing. My attorney has a copy of the letter in his files. If the rents are not paid promptly, you will go into default on your lease. If you do so, I shall not hesitate to have you evicted and then to rent your shop to someone else. Think about the consequences of your actions. Now, if you will excuse me, I'm in danger of being late for Church."

"You're going to be in grave danger," Jim growled as he approached her waving his fist. "I'm sick of this. Sick of you with your sanctimonious ways. You think you are so much better than the rest of us poor mortals." Then he started to take a swing at her.

A man came up from nowhere and caught Jim's fist. "I wouldn't do that if I were you," the second man growled.

"Who the hell are you?" Jim demanded.

"Someone you don't want to antagonize," he said lowly. Then he turned to Edwina and spoke in rapid

German, "*Fraulein* Doctor Johnson, please be on your way, I will deal with this person."

"This isn't any of your concern," Edwina said.

"On the contrary, this is what I'm paid to do. *Herr* Baron von Bruner would have my head on a platter if I let anything bad happen to you," the big man said firmly, retaining the German.

"I see. I shall be speaking to *Herr* von Bruner on this matter."

"I shall tell him to expect your call."

"You will not have the chance. Good day."

Edwina dug out her cell phone from her purse and punched in Klaus's number from memory. She walked on, quickly. The same very formal sounding male voice answered the phone.

"This is Edwina Johnson, again. Let me speak with Klaus, please, or if he's still on his conference call, leave him a message to return my call on my mobile number, as soon as possible."

"The first conference call scheduled for today ended two minutes ago. I shall connect you immediately," the man said.

"Edwina?" Klaus asked a long moment later.

"Just what do you think you are doing, Klaus?"

"In what regard?" he asked carefully.

"In what regard?" she echoed back incredulously, her voice rising half an octave. "In regard to the bodyguard you've put on me."

"Are you uninjured?" Klaus asked in concern. "Edwina, are you injured?"

Edwina kept walking. "Am I uninjured? Yes. I am relatively unharmed, apart from a bruise or two. But I'm angrier with you than I believe I've ever been at anyone else in my entire life. How dare you presume to place bodyguards in my service without telling me?"

"You would never have discovered Hans if you had not needed his intervention. He is better than that," he said quietly. "What happened, Edwina?"

"Ask your guard dog, or is he a watch dog? Is he here to guard me or to spy on me?"

"He is there for your safety and protection alone. Tell me what happened."

"I'm sure that your employee will give you a full report in vivid detail. Call him off, Klaus. I don't like bodyguards under the best of conditions."

"On the contrary, I believe that I shall redouble the protection on you. If Hans has to make his presence known, then you need someone else with you to keep you safe."

"You are an absolutely impossible man," she said in frustration.

"I take care of the people who belong to me. I believe I have told you that before."

"I don't belong to you," she denied hotly.

"Don't you?" he demanded. "Edwina, don't you belong to me, just as I belong to you?"

Without answering him, she disconnected the telephone call and shut off her cell phone. Then she dropped the phone back into her handbag.

The utter gall of the man!

She kept walking.

His. Did she want to be his? What did he want, beside the obvious?

Edwina felt her face grow warm with the remembrance of the dream. He'd confirmed that the details of the setting were accurate. No one could have that large of an imagination that she should get that many details right. So this had been another foretelling dream. It sent shivers down her spine.

There had been talk of eternity, of decisions, of a price to be paid for an eternity. Somehow, she didn't believe that to be hyperbole. She had no idea what it all meant. But it troubled her. She recalled his tone of voice in an earlier conversation when he spoke to her about the price of immortality. What was the price of immortality? How and why was this in his power to grant?

She tried to put all this out of her mind as she walked into the Church. But she couldn't get her mind off it. Neither the words of the liturgy nor the music made any impression on her mind. She was too preoccupied with her own thoughts, with thinking about the dream and Klaus. So when everyone else was going forward to receive Communion Edwina ducked out the back. She walked to the parking garage where she kept her car.

It was obvious to Edwina that she was being followed and not just by a single man. She didn't like it but she knew that she wasn't going to do anything about it. Until Klaus called them off they were quite likely to stay with her.

She didn't want to go out to Grandmother's house. The family always gathered there on Sundays for lunch. Any family member who was in the area and didn't come to Grandmother's for lunch was bound to hear about it from several fronts. Given the surprise party for her

Grandmother scheduled for Monday night, this gathering was likely to be mostly the aunts and uncles. Having most of the cousins suddenly blow into town would give away the surprise. Edwina was tempted to give this luncheon a miss. Skipping the inquisition wasn't worth the trouble that would come her way in terms of her aunts and uncles interfering in her life. Yet, she was tempted not to go, anyway.

"Yeah, EE, that's your problem. You have never given into temptation until recently," she muttered to herself as she started her car. "But, maybe, it's time you began to do that more often."

Chapter Six

Louella, the housekeeper, met Edwina at the door to Grandmother's house and took her coat. "She ain't going to like your coming without your gentleman friend," Louella warned.

"Then, she won't like it. It's beyond my power to change," Edwina dismissed. "How is she, really, Louella?"

"Same way she always is. The arthritis in her left hip bothers her something terrible. She doesn't complain but she doesn't move too good when it's acting up. And that's most of the time these days. She doesn't climb stairs anymore and she doesn't walk any further than she has to."

"Is she taking her anti-inflammatory and pain medication?"

"Under protest."

"As long as she takes the pills."

When Edwina walked into drawing room, she saw that all of her mother's brothers and sisters were present, but only two of her cousins Emily and Marie. Still, that didn't surprise her. If everyone who was in town had come, their grandmother would have more than a hint about her surprise birthday party on Monday.

"You've come alone, child," Grandmother observed in disappointment.

Edwina nodded. "I have indeed, Grandmother."

"Where's your gentleman friend, *Herr* Baron von Bruner?" Grandmother demanded.

"He had previous commitments as I believe I told you on the telephone this morning dear. We do not live in one another's pockets Klaus and I. He does have a life of his own as I do."

Grandmother wasn't pleased. Edwina could see that on the older woman's face. "We shall attempt to have Sunday lunch with him at some future date then."

"I do think you might want to wait on that to see if this relationship becomes serious, first, Grandmother."

The old woman laughed softly. "In other words, child, you don't want your battle-axe of a grandmother to scare him off?"

Edwina smiled as she sat down in a chair across the room from her grandmother. "It would take a great deal more than a few nosy relatives to scare Klaus away. He's entirely too strong willed to let a little opposition get in the way of anything he wants."

Grandmother chuckled. "Then, the two of you should be quite well matched, indeed, Granddaughter. You've never been scared of anything."

"Oh I wouldn't say that," Edwina replied lowly. "There is an old woman of my near acquaintance who has always inspired at least awe, if not fear, in me."

The old woman smiled as the clock chimed off half past the hour. "Falderal. It is time for luncheon. Shall we go in?"

Over the soup, Edwina's aunts and uncles began the inquisition she had known would be forthcoming. Edwina answered their questions over the soup and half way through the main course. Then she reached the end of her patience.

"I am thirty-five years old, Uncle. I have learned to recognize fortune hunters by now," Edwina said quietly, "As have the rest of my cousins. None of us need any of you to continue to interfere in our private lives. We are all in our late twenties to mid thirties, far older than any of you were when you wed. None of us are children. We are all responsible, productive, adults—the lot of us. Get used to that fact. And stop treating us as a pack of unruly children. It is really quite unnerving."

"Here, here," Cousin Emily, who at thirty-one was the headmistress of a private school, said meaningfully.

Cousin Marie added with a small laugh, "They're simply giving you the same attention that they've always given us when we've engaged in our first *affairs de cor*. No man, or woman, is good enough in their minds for the members of our generation of the family. Forget love. The union must be 'suitable'."

Cousin Emily cleared her throat. "Well, you have to admit Marie, you've gone a good job of proving men 'unsuitable' for your cousins over the years by stealing them away."

"Any man who can be stolen isn't worth having," Marie replied thoughtfully.

"I'll agree with that," Emily answered, with an edge of old pain to her voice.

Edwina still hurt for her cousin Emily. Marie had "stolen" away three of Emily's beaux, two of whom had been engaged to Emily. And then Marie had summarily and rather publicly dumped them. However, Emily's Jeff hadn't given Marie more than a cursory glance.

Personally, Edwina thought that Emily and Jeff should have married some time ago. They were perfect for one another.

"So, shall I go after your gentleman friend, Winnie?" Marie offered.

"Marie, I'm not worried about Klaus," Edwina said.

"Not even the slightest bit?" her cousin asked.

"Only in that Klaus has assigned bodyguards to me."

"You picked a good family with whom to make an alliance, Edwina. I wholeheartedly approve," Grandmother said. "I am satisfied with this alliance. It is suitable. There is no need for anyone to put the man to the test."

"Why would he put bodyguards on you?" Marie asked in puzzlement.

Edwina shook her head negatively. "He obviously doesn't believe that I can take care of myself."

"He doesn't know you very well, Winnie," Marie replied mischievously.

"Or he doesn't trust you and the bodyguards are spies reporting your comings and goings," Uncle Lawrence, the attorney in the family, offered, "I don't like this at all Edwina."

"I've had that thought Uncle," Edwina admitted. "I don't find the possibility pleasant either."

"Not a good way to start a relationship my dear," Uncle Lawrence replied, "It's a sign of a controlling, possibly abusive, person."

"Or a mark of prudence. He's a wealthy man with enemies. It's not outside of the scope of possibility that someone could want to get to him through me," Edwina allowed. "If I accept his proposal I'll have to get used to bodyguards. This is just the way that it is. He lives with high security surrounding him."

"Were the bodyguards that obvious that you have noticed them?" Emily asked in concern.

"No. I didn't notice them at all until one of the guards intervened this morning as one of my tenants got physical with me."

"How physical?" Uncle Richard demanded.

"My arm is still sore from where Jim grabbed me. It's bruised. But it's nothing serious enough to require medical attention. Don't concern yourself with it, Uncle."

"This is the tenant who believes his shop to be haunted by poltergeists?" Uncle Lawrence demanded.

"Same one. There was a small fire in his shop last night that the man claims was caused by supernatural forces."

"A fire?" her grandmother asked in concern.

"It was nothing. The alarms picked it up. I went downstairs and Klaus put it out."

"Ah, Klaus was with you last night," Marie observed.

"We were sitting in my library having a glass of wine after coming back from a late supper when the alarm went off if that was any of your concern," Edwina said pointedly.

"In your library, in front of the fire, with the lights dimmed. A very romantic setting, Winnie..." Marie said quietly with a smile on her face. "I can see it now."

Edwina smiled. "You always did have an active imagination."

"It runs in the family," Marie said pointedly.

"Your tenant's unstable. It's time to get him some help," Uncle Lawrence said, "Before he hurts himself or someone else. I'll draft the complaint. You will need to sign it to get him put under thirty days psychiatric observation. Your liability insurance will handle any repercussions from signing the complaint."

"I'm not quite convinced that this is anything except an elaborate attempt at extortion," Edwina replied. "He told me that he wanted me to pay to relocate his shop into a major mall and to pay his first quarter's rent."

"So, what did you tell him?" Uncle Lawrence demanded.

"I told him that it wasn't my responsibility to set him up in another retail location. Then I repeated my offer to have the shop, the whole building in fact, blessed in an effort to chase away the supposed spirits. He called that superstitious nonsense, and then tried to hit me. That's when the bodyguard intervened. If the bodyguard, Hans, had stayed out of this, I would have handled it myself."

Marie laughed. "I've seen you 'handle' situations. I never understood why Aunt Anne and Uncle Vernon made you take all those years of martial arts classes until that evening in Paris fourteen years ago when we were accosted…"

Uncle James looked at his daughter in open concern, "I don't believe I've heard this story."

"It's nothing. There was no harm done, Uncle," Edwina dismissed sharply. Why Marie had brought that up now was beyond Edwina's understanding.

"Except to the men," Marie added, mischief in her eyes. "Winnie left them both in a heap on the street, in too much pain to continue to bother us any further. I wasn't scared until each of them pulled a big wicked-looking knife. But Winnie handled them with moves that I hadn't seen except in martial arts films."

"Need I remind you, Cousin, that it was your idea not to worry the parents with this particular story?" Edwina asked quietly. "And now you bring that story to their attention?"

"It's ancient history," Marie countered.

"Not to us, it isn't," Uncle James said firmly. "What exactly happened?"

Edwina sighed. "Not much. Marie and I were out for the evening. We went to a disco. A couple of weird guys followed us out onto the street without invitation. Marie and I were never in much danger."

"Knives tend to mean that there is plenty of danger, Edwina," Uncle James corrected.

"Neither of the boys had any skill with a knife, Uncle. Anyone with any skill with a knife would have handled the cutlery differently. They were half-inebriated and uncoordinated. The intent was merely to frighten. There was really truly little danger."

"Any danger is too much," Uncle James stated flatly. "And I suspect the intention was to frighten to the point of gaining submission to their advances."

Edwina sighed. "Probably…But like I said, they were just drunk enough to lose their inhibitions. It made them a little reckless. There wasn't really much danger there. My only concern was how much pain I was going to have to inflict on them before they began to see it as a deterrent. They were fairly well anaesthetized with drink as it was."

"Not much danger?" Uncle James demanded.

"Life is a matter of a certain amount of danger," Edwina replied. "It can't be helped. The only way to totally avoid danger is never to interact with people in any way, shape, or form. And that's too high a price to pay for a little safety."

"Just how much damage did you finally do to the men in order to defend yourself and Marie?" her uncle demanded.

Edwina sighed. "I didn't stick around to do a full physical examination. But I know that one of them ended up with a broken knee. I think I merely dislocated both knees of the other one. Neither of them was in any shape to chase us. And Marie and I got out of there rather quickly."

"I see," her uncle replied.

"I shall have to thank Herr von Bruner for his thoughtfulness in looking after my granddaughter by providing her with bodyguards," Grandmother said, quietly, changing the subject. "And I will let him know that my granddaughter is well capable of caring for herself."

"Where are these bodyguards now?"

"Outside. I saw them following me here."

Uncle Lawrence rose from the table without comment. He walked out of the house, closing the door behind him.

Edwina sighed. "I do wish he hadn't done that."

"Your family loves you, Granddaughter."

"I know."

Uncle Lawrence came back in. He resumed his place at the table. "Two men?" he asked Edwina.

"Yes, Uncle. Now, can we, please, drop the subject of my guards?" Edwina asked. "Marie, have you designed any outrageous fashions lately?"

"Of course," Marie agreed.

"Good. I want to see the portfolio. I need a few new things for evenings."

"If you are seeing a man like Klaus von Bruner, Winnie, I would say so. The man is as rich as they come. He's been known to squire about any number of beautiful women, including some of my models," Marie agreed.

Edwina sighed. "If Klaus is used to beautiful women like Marie's models, what is he doing with me?" she asked herself only in her mind.

Marie must have misread the expression on her face, because she hurried into further explanation. "None of the girls have had any complaints about him. One or two even imagined herself in love with him. I can ask them about his personal life, if you would like. Just to make certain that he has no… unusual… preferences."

Edwina found her face growing warm. "Marie. Thank you. I know that you mean well."

"Yet you would just as soon find out about the man's preferences yourself?" Marie said with a wicked smile on her face.

"I trust him," Edwina said simply. And she was surprised that she did.

Marie looked at her and smiled. "I have five gowns in the Spring line that would be perfect on you. They're understated and beautiful."

Edwina sipped her water. "The last time you sent me an evening gown that you described that way, the neckline was a deep V that ended at my navel, there was a slit up the side that ended at my hip, and the back of the halter necked dress—if you can call it that—consisted of little more than the skirt. It showed my kidney dimples, for heaven's sake. There was no way to wear anything under the gown."

"It was lined. Nothing showed through. You looked extraordinarily lovely in it! Especially when you wore Aunt Anne's emeralds with it," Marie replied. "I never understood why you wouldn't wear the gown in public."

"Someone once described me as a 'colorless lab rat'," Edwina answered thoughtfully. "In many ways, that's what I am."

Marie cleared her throat pointedly. "Pah, if you are it is only because you've chosen to hide behind that terrible façade," she said tightly.

Edwina shrugged. "Perhaps."

"I'll send the gowns to you by the end of the week, if I have to cut and sew them myself," Marie promised.

"Thanks."

"Your measurements are still the same?"

"After lunch, you can retake them."

It was almost three by the time that Edwina had left her grandmother's house.

The car with the bodyguards followed her to the nursery. She went into the offices and changed clothes in the rest room, changing into a work jumpsuit, chore coat, and boots. She didn't intend to do any real work, but she wanted to walk the acreage and look at the stock, check the green houses, and begin to get some inspiration for Klaus' garden. She was prepared to tag any plant that appealed to her for possible inclusion in the garden.

Besides that, she enjoyed just being out where young things grew. It was peaceful here on Sunday afternoon. Starting the coming weekend, the nursery would be open on Sunday afternoon from noon until three to meet the needs of hobby gardeners. Edwina didn't like letting the nursery be open on Sunday, but that was the way that this business was.

Hans, the bodyguard, was waiting for her when she came out of the offices. "*Fraulein* Doctor," he began.

"Come along, since you're coming. Just don't get in my way."

He smiled. "*Danke.*"

She stayed there on the nursery grounds until sunset, picking out plants and puttering in her greenhouses. Then she changed clothes. Hans drove her back to town. He insisted. The other car with the other driver followed them.

When she got back to the shop, she noticed that Klaus' car was parked on the street.

"You've had a long day," Klaus greeted her.

He was so handsome. Just looking at her took his breath away. He wore another of those immaculately tailored suits under his overcoat. Every inch of him proclaimed him to be a man of wealth and breeding. She wanted to think herself unimpressed by his obvious wealth. Yet, she wasn't convinced of the truth of that.

"How did your conference call go?"

"I've had four of those today. They all went well enough."

"I'm glad."

"You've made your decision about us."

"What makes you think I have done that?"

"Haven't you?" Klaus asked carefully.

"No, I don't believe I have."

"Then I have the pleasure of attempting to convince you," Klaus said with a smile.

Lord, how she loved his smile!

"Are you going to invite me inside?" he asked.

"I don't believe that would be wise, given how we react to one another."

"Then, will you come to dinner with me?"

"Yes. That I will do."

"Shall we walk? Or would you rather go someplace other than one of the restaurants in this neighborhood?"

"Do you like Chinese food?"

He smiled. "Cantonese, Mandarin, or Szechwan?"

"Mandarin and Szechwan. There's a good place a couple of blocks over. It's a nice walk."

"Then, by all means, let's go. This time, no pretenses that this is anything except a date. You and I both know that we're not going to be able to dance around this desire for very long."

Edwina looked at him for a long moment. "Klaus, you're rushing me and I'm not comfortable with it."

"I would suggest that you get comfortable with it. I am not going away."

She looked at him. "Klaus, I don't know what to do with you."

He laughed. "Would you like some suggestions?" he teased her mercilessly.

"Only if the first one is finding some dinner."

Klaus held out his arm to her. "Come and walk with me. Show me where this restaurant is."

The restaurant was not overly busy, but it was busy enough for a Sunday night well after the regular dinner rush. Klaus ordered in what sounded to Edwina like fluent Chinese. He and the waitress had a prolonged discussion in that language. But Edwina's understanding of Chinese was limited to items from a menu.

What came when the food arrived was nothing like Edwina had ever had off the regular menu.

"Where did you learn Chinese?" Edwina asked between spicy bites.

"I do a fair amount of business with the People's Republic and Taiwan. It's only prudent to speak the language," he dismissed.

"How many languages do you speak?"

"A few," he dismissed.

"Klaus," she asked in German, "which languages do you speak?"

"German, Dutch, English, Italian, Mandarin Chinese, Japanese, and Korean," he answered in German. "And I can muddle through Flemish, Norwegian, Danish, French, and Spanish when I have to. What languages do you speak?"

"English, German, Russian, Spanish, Greek, and French. I can muddle through Polish, Ukrainian, and Romanian, if I have to. I can read Italian but haven't been around enough native speakers to have the spoken word be anywhere near fluent."

"We could solve that easily enough. We could go live in Europe for a few years. I have a house in Northern

Italy," he offered in German. "It's a beautiful place, out in the countryside, quite peaceful."

"My grandmother says that one of her great-grandmother's sisters, Regina, married into the von Bruner family from Bavaria," she said in English, side-stepping that offer.

Klaus smiled slightly. "The Schloss is in Bavaria. It's a beautiful place. But it belongs to another era. I'd have to check the family history. I do know that several of my ancestors married Englishwomen. I'm serious about the offer of marriage, Edwina. We could have a very good life together."

"A Schloss. Then the 'von' actually denotes the rank of a Baron."

Klaus sighed. "Yes, for whatever that means in the modern world. I prefer to be known for my own accomplishments, not for my ancestors. But, if the title means something to you, then I would be happy to call you Baroness."

"We need to get to know one another a lot better than we do before I'd even consider marriage. And I'm far too American to be terribly impressed by titles of nobility."

He smiled. "What would it take for you to be terribly impressed?"

"Ah, I don't think that I'll tell you that. It would give you an unfair advantage."

"I'll take any advantage I can get," he said with a smile.

"Shame on you, Klaus. You haven't struck me as a man who would take advantage of a defenseless woman."

"There isn't a defenseless woman sitting at this table."

"And how would you know that?"

"Hans tells me that you are obviously well trained in martial arts. He said that you were about to hand your tenant his head in a hand basket this morning. Hans' assessment is that you could handle anything short of an attack by firearms with ease."

"I hope I never have to find out about that."

"I hope not either. But it is good to know that I don't have to worry about your ability to defend yourself in most situations."

"Thanks."

"I spoke with your Uncle Richard this afternoon."

"You know Uncle Richard?"

"We've met."

"And what did Uncle Richard have to say when he spoke to you?"

"Not nearly as much as your Uncles Lawrence, James, Thomas, Frederick, or Robert did."

Edwina rolled her eyes. "Is there anyone in my family that you haven't heard from today?"

"I received phone calls from six uncles, five aunts, and a grandmother. Is there anyone else I should have heard from?" Klaus replied with amusement in his voice.

"Oh, let's see… there are my forty-five cousins."

"You did say that you were from a large family," Klaus replied in a bemused tone.

"It's a mixed blessing at times."

"Yes," he replied with an edge of something indefinable in his voice. "We can discuss our respective families over dinner each evening this week."

"The shop closes at nine."

He nodded. "Then I will be there promptly to take you to dinner, beginning tomorrow night."

"Not tomorrow. It's my grandmother's birthday. There is a big surprise party for her at the country club where she's been a member since it was organized. I do suspect that someone has disclosed it to her by now. But we're all pretending that it's a surprise."

"You're closing the shop?"

"No. I've got part time help come in to cover for me."

"Yet you are unwilling to leave your shop in the hands of part time help on a regular basis," Klaus said quietly.

"I've got the venture on a very tight budget right now. I have part time shop help for only thirty hours a week. More than that, I really can't afford. And I only have that to allow me the ability to meet with clients and prospective clients during the hours that the shop is open."

"And perhaps to give you some time to work on your own projects?" he offered.

"Perhaps," she agreed.

Klaus nodded. "I'd like to read your business plan sometime, and run the numbers. Maybe we can find a way of letting you have more time off."

"Trust me, I've run the figures until I'm sick of running them. I didn't go into business blindly."

"Knowing you, I didn't think you did. How many years have you been plotting this venture of yours?"

"I started playing with the idea about seventeen years ago in a business class as an undergraduate."

"So, this has been a long time goal of yours. It's not just something you've used as an escape-valve after you found you didn't like working in biotechnology."

"I love biotechnology. But the world isn't really ready to face the full ethical implications of the science."

"You're still working on the narcotic project, aren't you?" he asked in rapid German.

"Klaus, I have no intention of discussing my work with you in any further detail. Especially not in public," she answered in equally rapid German.

"This is dangerous, Edwina. You run risks."

"Any risk is one that I willingly undertake, Klaus. Now, let's speak in English and about only non-controversial subjects."

Klaus laughed. "There is no such thing with us, my dear," he answered in English.

"Your garden."

"How many acres of nursery ground do you have?"

"I own a majority position in the corporation that owns one hundred and sixty acres of ground."

"That's a lot of trees and shrubs."

"It's enough to provide support for the landscaping business."

"And it gives you a great deal of greenhouse space."

"That too, although most of the greenhouse space is occupied right now with bedding plants for the spring planting season or lilies for the Easter season. Those sort of things are a profit center for the spring season."

Klaus nodded. "Most of it?"

She glanced at him over the top of her eyeglasses. Then she changed the subject. "This was really delicious. Thank you."

"Have you eaten all you're going to?"

"I guess I have. It was all very good. Just there was enough food here to feed five or six people."

"Try a little more. You need to fuel up."

"I do? For what?"

"We're going dancing."

"Klaus, I'm not dressed for dancing."

"You look fine to me."

Edwina smiled and shook her head negatively. "Thanks. I wasn't fishing for compliments."

"No. You never do."

"I wouldn't say 'never'," she replied quietly.

"When was the last time that you fished for a compliment?"

Edwina thought for a long moment. "I really can't remember."

"That's what I thought. You are entirely comfortable with yourself."

"I doubt that any of us are entirely comfortable with ourselves, Klaus," she answered thoughtfully. "I know that I'm not."

He smiled and took her hand. "Come on, Edwina, come dancing with me. I want to hold you in my arms. Dancing provides an excuse. We could dance all night."

"No. I couldn't. I have a piece of property to walk off with my staff first thing in the morning. Something about a small commission of a garden to be planted for a German."

Klaus smiled. "That can wait."

"No. I don't think it can," she said remembering her dream. The plantings had been underway. The sooner this began, the sooner... Edwina's face grew hot.

"You're blushing again. What are you thinking?"

Edwina shook her head negatively. "Nothing really."

"Somehow, I think it was more than nothing."

With a sigh, Edwina admitted, "Klaus, I'm trying to work this out in my mind. Just give me some time."

"Tell me about this dream you had that was set in my bedroom."

"No. I don't think so."

"Do you normally dream in such accurate detail as you described to me?"

"More often than I care to."

"They aren't always good dreams?"

"No."

"What was the worst?" he asked.

She was quiet for a long moment, uncertain of whether to tell him about this or not. "The night before my parents died."

Klaus looked at her. "You saw them die in your dream?"

"I saw the accident," she said. "I got up, wrote down the description of my dream in my journal, like I always do when it's a profoundly real dream, with the description of the dream and sketches of what I saw."

"Did you sketch last night's dream?" Klaus demanded.

"Of course. I always document my dreams."

"Why?"

"To separate out the fantasy from the reality so that I can stay sane."

"I want to see those sketches."

"My journal is my own concern. It is none of anyone else's business."

"Then sketch the room for me, *now!*" he ordered with some urgency in his voice.

Edwina looked at him. She sighed. "I haven't any paper."

Klaus called over the waitress. Less than a minute later, she returned with a few sheets of typing paper. "Now, you have paper. Show me what you saw in your dream."

She removed a pen from her purse and quickly produced two sketches for him of the room from different vantage points. She didn't look up at him.

Then she handed him the drawings. He looked at them, at her, and then back at the sketches once more.

"How do you explain your dreams, Edwina Elizabeth?" Klaus asked gently.

"I don't. Is the room accurate?"

"I ordered those chairs a month ago. They'll be delivered after the new carpet goes down," Klaus said. "But, yes, the room accurately reflects what it will be in a couple of weeks. What else did you dream?"

"I'm not entirely comfortable discussing it."

"Why not? Edwina, the dream was about us, wasn't it?"

"Definitely."

"And you said it was a good dream," he urged.

"It was a profoundly sensual dream."

"Then why would you be hesitant to discuss it?"

"I'm not entirely comfortable with the paranormal."

"Had much experience with the paranormal, aside from dreams?" he asked carefully.

"Aside from my resident ghost, no," she said flippantly.

Edwina could sense the tension in him.

"Your resident ghost? Are you joking?" he asked tightly.

"One of my tenants swears up and down that the building is haunted."

'That's not the same thing as a resident ghost," he said in concern.

Edwina shrugged.

"The Schloss allegedly has a couple of ghosts," he said easily. "I've never seen them, but the staff swears that they are there. Then again, it would be an odd castle that didn't have some sort of legend like that."

"Do you believe in ghosts, Klaus?" Edwina asked quietly.

"I believe that there are evil things who sometimes masquerade as ghosts. I have seen something in the house in Madrid. The figure was ethereal. The room dropped at least ten degrees in temperature when I saw it. He spoke to me. Said his name was Luis."

Edwina sighed. "How did that make you feel to talk to a shade?"

"Like I was losing my mind."

"I can identify with that. So what did you do?"

"Called a cousin of mine who is a priest. And I asked him to come. He did."

"Did it get rid of Luis?"

"Yes."

Edwina sighed. "I offered to pay for a priest to come to bless the building, when this tenant began complaining about spirits in his shop. I probably ought to make the arrangements. I've been hesitant to do that because I didn't want to raise the issue of something supernatural. It's not a topic usually raised within the normal areas of conversation."

"You say you haven't seen anything malevolent," Klaus said carefully. "How about anything benign or even neutral?"

"You should have taken your degrees in law instead of in medicine and biochemistry, Klaus."

"You have done a little research on me," he said quietly.

"Just to find out who you were. It took me all of five minutes on the Internet."

"Have you seen anything unusual in the building?"

Edwina sighed. "Just every time I look into a mirror," she teased.

Klaus smiled at her. "I'm serious."

She didn't know whether to say anything or not. She sighed. "There is one presence. She calls herself 'Catherine' and she pops in at odd times. The room chills and there she is. First few times I saw her, I thought I was going to die of fright. I've gradually gotten used to her. I ignore her most of the time."

"She didn't pop in last night."

"Yes, she did, after you left the bathroom."

"About the time the cats howled?"

"They always yowl when she pops in."

"Would you like for me to make arrangements with my cousin for him to come? He deals with the paranormal every day. That's his area of expertise. He's technically assigned to the Congregation for Divine Worship and the Discipline of the Sacraments and has an office in the Vatican."

"That would be your cousin Wilhelm?" she asked carefully.

"You know Willie?" Klaus asked in surprise.

"No."

He looked at her for the longest time. "How deep did your research on me go, Edwina?"

"This wasn't research. I had a dream about ten years ago in which I met Wilhelm. I'd forgotten about that until I went through my journals the other day."

Klaus looked at her carefully. "You met Willie in your dreams? In what context?"

Edwina felt her face grow hot again. "It's not significant, Klaus."

"If you're blushing it is significant."

"He was officiating at a wedding."

"Whose wedding?"

"Ours."

Klaus was silent for a long moment. He sat back and looked at her for a long time. "You have been dreaming of me for some time then?" he asked carefully.

"You could say that."

"How long have you had dreams about me?"

"A long time."

"How long? The ten years you mentioned?"

"Longer than that."

Klaus was silent for a moment as he tried to absorb that. "How many dreams have you had about me, Edwina?"

"Thousands."

"Have they been pleasant dreams?"

"For the most part."

"Is it the same dream or are they different?"

"There haven't been two that have been the same."

"Then how can you say that you do not know me?"

"Dreams aren't real, Klaus."

"Willie should be happy to come to help you deal with the problems with ghosts."

"Bringing in an outside 'expert' might step on a few ecclesiastical toes. I know that the Archdiocese has an exorcist on staff. I don't know who he is. But I know that the Cardinal has one on staff. It would be a small matter to ask the Archdiocese for assistance in this matter. Of course, it would likely have to be channeled through the parish."

"It wouldn't step on any toes if my cousin came for our wedding. I can arrange for this to happen."

"It's not even Lent, yet, Klaus. I don't think I can wait on this until after Easter."

"Ash Wednesday is in two weeks. We could set up a wedding before then."

Edwina laughed nervously, remembering the Mardi Gras notation. "If we did, people would be counting the weeks between our marriage and the birth of a first child."

Klaus smiled broadly. "Let them. That is the least of our problems."

"Oh, Klaus!"

He brought a velvet box out of his pocket and handed it to her.

She opened the box and looked at the ring. It was the ring from her dream- a narrow platinum band with a marquis cut emerald. Then she looked at him, panic on her face. "I didn't tell you about this."

Klaus looked at her in concern. "Edwina?"

"I saw this ring on my hand in several of the dreams. Along with a wedding band set with diamonds."

He brought another box out of his pocket. "This ring?" he demanded as he opened the second box.

Edwina looked at the rings, and then at him. "Those are the rings."

He was quiet for a moment. "I bought this ring yesterday before I came to see you. It was in my pocket. Large diamonds are so cold. I thought that the emerald would suit you better. It matches the fire in your eyes. I was going to give them to you last night. But we rather became distracted, one way and another."

Edwina looked at the ring. "What do you want from me, Klaus?"

Klaus looked at her carefully. "What do you think I want from you?"

"You've been known to date truly beautiful women."

Klaus looked at her as though she had just sprouted two heads. "Yes. I have. Yet none of them hold a candle to you. None of them engaged my heart and my mind. I was torn with none of them between the joint desires to ravish and to protect."

"Just to ravish."

"I am a man, Edwina, who has a large sexual appetite. It's part of who I am. It's been a very long time since I was an innocent."

"So, why are you here with me?"

"Edwina, nothing in this world or the next would make me a happier man than to have you as my wife. Will you please marry me?"

"I want to say 'yes'."

"Then say it."

"I need time, Klaus. Marriage is a lifetime commitment. I need to be sure."

He called over the waitress and paid the bill. He handed her a one hundred dollar bill and obviously told her to keep the change. That had definitely won him welcome again. "Since you won't go dancing with me at least let me walk you home."

They walked in silence for several minutes.

"Did I make you angry, Klaus?"

"No, my dear. I am not angry. I certainly cannot blame you for being cautious. We have not known one another that long."

"No. We haven't. Thank you for being reasonable."

"I am generally reasonable."

"I do love you, Klaus." *And I've loved you for a long time*, she thought but didn't dare say.

He smiled. "That's a beginning. I'm not a patient man, Edwina."

"That's because you've always had beautiful women at your beck and call," she offered dryly.

"Why, Edwina, that sounds almost jealous," he observed.

She shrugged slightly. "Given your dating history, I have to wonder what you see in me."

"Insecurity? From you, my dear?" Klaus asked in disbelief.

"I'm as human as the next woman."

"And twice as interesting."

Edwina laughed quietly. "Right," she dismissed.

They arrived back at her shop. "Are you going to invite me in for a cup of coffee?" he asked hopefully.

"No. I'm not. Thank you for dinner, Klaus. It was lovely."

"It was my pleasure."

"Well, goodnight."

"Not yet, my dear," he said quietly as they stood in the doorway to the shop. He gathered her into his arms. "You wouldn't send me away without a good-night kiss, would you?"

She kissed his cheek. "Good night, Klaus."

"Vixen," he murmured just before he captured her lips with his.

As before, the passion flared immediately. His passion demanded her response, which she freely gave. Passion built on passion.

"Edwina," he whispered in her ear, "Invite me inside."

"No, Klaus. That wouldn't be a good idea," she said as she stepped back from him.

"It sounds good to me."

"Can you settle for coffee?"

"No."

She looked at him for a long moment and finally came to the decision that had been bothering her for days. "Then I suppose that you should come up."

He didn't have to be asked twice.

Chapter Seven

Edwina let herself into the shop and made her way up the stairs to her apartment. Klaus followed her.

"Go on into the study. Light the fire. I'll be with you in a few moments," she said quietly.

"Edwina, you needn't be so nervous."

"I just need ten minutes. Make yourself at home. Coffee or something stronger?"

"Coffee would be fine. Would you like for me to make it?"

Edwina smiled at him. "Sure...if you want to. I keep the coffee beans in the freezer. The grinder is on the counter. Just put the ground beans in a filter and put that into the basket of the drip machine. It's hooked into the water supply, so just hit the start button. The coffee will be ready in a couple of minutes."

He smiled at her. "Leave it to you to take your coffee that seriously."

"I live on caffeine."

He chuckled. "Caffeine is a food group?"

"It's an essential of life. Excuse me for a few minutes."

She left him and went to the bathroom, brushed her teeth, washed her face, took down her hair and began to brush it. The room temperature dropped ten degrees. When she turned around, Catherine was standing there.

"You're playing with fire, Edwina."

"If I were, the room would be much warmer," Edwina told the shade.

"This is not a joking matter!"

"Go away, Catherine."

"That creature, that von Bruner, is going to destroy you, Edwina. He cares about nothing and no one except himself."

"That's not true, Catherine."

"You've fallen under that creature's spell!"

"I've fallen under no one's spell."

"He has a seductive charm. But then again, beasts of his ilk do. It's one of their major and defining characteristics."

"What are you talking about?"

"He's a creature of the night, Edwina."

"What do you mean?"

"Have you ever seen him in the daytime?"

"What does that have to do with anything? He is intolerant of UV."

"Oh, he's intolerant of UV. That's putting it mildly. What was your first thought when you saw him for the very first time?" the shade demanded.

"Again, what does that have to do with anything?"

"Edwina, you have a good sense of what is dangerous and what is not. What was your first impression of the creature?"

"Catherine, go away."

"Not this time. You have to listen. I won't be here much longer to help you. I'll have to be moving on soon. You have to listen to me. Edwina, please!"

"Where would you go?"

"Wherever I'm sent. It's my duty. I go and I do the bidding of the Master."

"And who is the Master?"

The shade looked at Edwina for a long moment. "You were raised in the Church. You know who the Master is. It is forbidden for any of us to speak the name. Now, listen to me, well, Edwina. I won't be with you much longer."

"I'm listening."

"Ask your grandmother to find the photograph of Regina and Johann von Bruner. It's among her copies of the family records. It's an old glass negative photo, so it's very fragile. But, look at it hard. Do it without much more delay. Time is of the essence. Nothing less than your immortal soul lies in the balance."

"And what will an old family photo prove?"

"That will be obvious when you see it, Edwina." And with that the shade blinked out.

Edwina picked up her hairbrush and finished brushing her hair. She needed to do something. Her hands were shaking. What could an old photograph show her? It didn't make any sense. A creature of the night? Of course, he functioned best at night. He wasn't the first man whom she had known who had a profound intolerance of UV radiation. It was rare, but there were several documented medical conditions for which an intolerance of UV was part of the list of complaints.

Edwina went to the closet and pulled out another of the caftans that Marie had given her over the years. This one was a rich emerald green silk.

Quickly, she took off her clothes and undergarments and pulled the caftan over her head. She took one more look in the mirror. Yes, that would do quite nicely. She grabbed a couple of thick beach towels and a bottle of infused herbal oil before she left the room.

Klaus had managed the coffee quite well. He had a tray sitting on the hearth of the fireplace. He'd found her stash of fancy cookies and had put some of those on a plate. Pillows were on the floor. Klaus was half reclining on the floor, propped up with pillows, looking into the fire. He'd taken off his shoes, socks, and suit coat. The only light in the room came from the soft glow of the gas log.

She was just about to him when he looked up at her. She watched him swallow hard as she knelt down beside him. She put down the towels and the bottle of oil.

"You are so incredibly beautiful. It makes my arms ache to hold you."

"Good. I'd hate to think I was the only one with that problem."

He reached up and grabbed a handful of her hair and gently—but decidedly—forced her head to his. The kiss was hungry, almost beyond hunger. Then he pulled away from her.

"What are the rules we are operating under tonight, Edwina?" he demanded.

"Are there rules? All I know is that I want you."

He smiled. "I've decided that I'm not going to let you have me unless you make an honest man of me," he teased.

"Are you a dishonest man?"

He chuckled. Then he continued to tease her, "I would be if I let you take what I have saved for the woman I will marry. So have a cup of coffee and we'll talk."

She poured both of them a cup of coffee then handed him his cup. He'd made it strong the way that she liked it. She finished her cup and replaced the china on the tray.

"Okay. We'll talk. Shall I tell you of the dreams I've had about us?"

"Only if they're fit for my maidenly ears," he teased.

Edwina snorted with her laughter. "On second thought," she said quietly as she crossed the room to him, "maybe I should just show you." As she spoke, her hands went to his necktie. "I don't know why men wear these things, they look so terribly uncomfortable." She pulled the tie loose from around his collar. Edwina smoothed the imported silk between her fingers, before she placed the tie down on the sofa cushion just behind her.

"You look comfortable with those bare feet. Are you wearing anything under that caftan?" Klaus asked quietly.

"Now, that's an interesting question. When we get a bit more equal in the clothing department, I might let you find out."

"Why, Doctor Johnson, I believe you have designs on my person," Klaus observed.

"You were duly warned, Doctor von Bruner. Yet you came here anyway."

"I did."

"I still like those shirts of yours," she told him as she began unfastening the studs. "But there are times I really wish they had zippers."

Klaus laughed boldly. "A bit impatient, Edwina?"

"Take off your shirt, Klaus, before I rip it off you," she said with mock menace.

"Help, I'm being ravished by a red haired wanton," he whispered.

"You know what they say, 'God helps those who help themselves'?"

"Then, I'm lost forever, because I can't help loving you."

"Take off your clothes, Klaus, and no one will get hurt," she teased.

"Oh, I'm terrified," he replied in mock fear.

She unfastened the cuff links on his shirt and pulled the partially unfastened shirt off over his head. "I still say you should be sculpted, immortalized in stone or bronze, so that people can enjoy the beauty of your form for a long time." She tossed the shirt on the sofa.

He smiled at her. "You really want to share me?"

"No. I'm greedy. I want you all to myself."

"I'm all yours."

"I've dreamed about this."

"Have you?" he demanded, suddenly serious.

"I have."

"Tell me about it."

"No. But I'll walk you through it. Take off your trousers and your boxers."

He stood and divested himself of his remaining clothing.

Edwina swallowed hard. Looking at him made her mouth dry. She spread out one of the big beach towels that she had brought in with her. "Lay down on your stomach."

He looked at her in disbelief. Then he complied.

Edwina pulled off her caftan over her head and threw that garment where Klaus could see it. She knelt, straddling his hips, and she poured a little oil in her hand.

"What are you doing?"

"Going to give you a massage. First, I'll work on your back and legs," she said as she began at his shoulders.

Touching him was nearly as exciting as being touched by him. She forced herself to breathe. She lectured herself in her mind to keep the touch therapeutic, to work on loosening up his muscles, relaxing him. Edwina tried very hard to ignore the sexual tension in her lower body, the heated moisture between her legs, and the heaviness in her breasts. Yet, her mind kept replaying the rest of the dream. She wondered if she would be bold enough to take what she wanted.

"Edwina!" Klaus moaned as she had almost finished working on his legs.

"Doesn't it feel good, Klaus?"

"You know that it does. You are pushing me to my limits, *Liebling*."

"Good. I want you to be wild for me. Roll over," she said as she moved to the side.

"Oh, I'm wild for you," he said as he reached for her.

"Talk is cheap."

He pulled her down atop him. Then he rolled over suddenly, bringing her beneath him. He kneed her thighs apart. "I'll try to be gentle."

"I won't break, Klaus," she said quietly as she shifted her body and rolled him over to his back. "But I also won't have you thinking that you've seduced me and worrying yourself into a state of guilt. This is my responsibility, Klaus."

He smiled at her. "I love you."

"I know," she said with a returning smile as she lowered herself slowly, guiding his erect penis into her vagina.

Klaus watched her face carefully as he felt her hymen give way. But she had closed her eyes and wasn't giving any indication with her expression of how she much or how little discomfort she was experiencing. She did expel a stream of air through her teeth after she finished slowly sheathing the hard, hot, length of his cock within her.

"How are you feeling?" he asked in concern.

She laughed quietly as she opened her eyes and looked at him. "I don't know. How am I feeling around you?"

"Like heaven."

"Good," she said as she squeezed her pelvic floor muscles around his penis. "I'd hate to think that only one of us was enjoying this."

"*Frau!*"

"Klaus!" she cried as he reached down and began to lightly stimulate her clitoris. It didn't take much additional stimulation to send her over the edge.

Klaus sat up and held her tightly as she climaxed.

"Wrap your legs around me," he instructed as she came down from her sensual high.

She complied.

"Hold onto me," he told her as he rose to his knees and then to his feet. He carried her to her bedroom.

Her bed was nothing more than a Queen sized mattress on a pedestal. The sheets and coverlet were turned down. He lowered her to the mattress and followed her down.

There were no words. There was no energy for further words. Klaus, leaning up on his elbows, began thrusting. Edwina looked up at him. The muscles of his upper arms and shoulders flexed and bunched as he braced himself over her. She knew that she had never seen anything as beautiful as this man loving her. And it was love, she realized. He was a considerate lover.

There were so many sensations bombarding her, Edwina could hardly keep up with them all. She met each of his thrusts with a lift of her hips. The tension in both of them built to a nearly unbearable level.

Edwina reached a second climax. She cried out his name a split second before the edges of her vision became blurry and everything went dark for a moment. When she came around, a short moment later, she could feel his penis still within her, throbbing as her pelvic muscles gave him strong contractions as a reward.

Then he collapsed upon her. He buried his face in her throat. Klaus thrust into her hard, deep, for five more strokes before his body stiffened. He cried out her name as she felt the hot pulsing of his climax.

Gently, Klaus rolled over onto his side and pulled Edwina into his embrace, snuggled tightly against him. He dropped kisses all over her face, brushing his lips over her forehead, cheeks, the tip of her nose, her mouth, her chin, and down her throat.

She had never felt so cherished or so tired.

Klaus lay there and looked at her as she dozed. He pulled the coverlet up over them.

He looked around the room, really looked, for the first time. She had called this room 'monastic' and that wasn't a bad descriptor. The bed was larger than any he had ever found in a monastery. But the furniture wasn't much more than functional. She was right about other aspects of the room seeming monastic. There was a crucifix hanging on the wall at her bed head. There was rosary on her night table. She was right about another part of her assessments. There were too many windows in this room for him to be able to spend the rest of the night with her here.

He looked at her face resting in sleep and smiled. He didn't think he would ever forget this moment. He had told her that he wanted to lay with her, watching her sleep the sleep of a woman well and truly loved.

He didn't like the rather ugly bruise on her arm. He made a mental note to have a long talk with her tenant Jim Douglass in that regard. That any man should lay hands on Edwina raised his anger. He lightly kissed her temple.

He watched her face as she smiled.

The house was full of people. The tall grandfather's clock in the foyer rang off ten thirty p.m. as she came down the stairs. A large Christmas tree stood by the curving gray marble staircase. There was a good deal of laughter coming from the large gathering room. A small group of adults whom she didn't know filled the gathering room and stood around a grand piano singing Christmas carols in German. Klaus was seated at the piano, playing those carols. There was a large fire crackling in the fireplace. Klaus looked up at her. She met his eyes. She felt her face grow warm because of the promising look in his eye.

"Klaus," one of the men said with a laugh in rapid German, "married to the woman for over two and one half years, and she still blushes when you look at her?"

Klaus finished the song and rose from the piano bench.

He came over to her. Lightly touching her face, he asked, "Is the baby asleep?"

"He finally closed his eyes and drifted off."

Klaus looked up. "You realize where you are standing?"

Edwina laughed softly. "I did hang the mistletoe, Klaus."

"You did, didn't you?" he teased. "So," he said as he took her into his arms. "Then you will just have to pay the penalty."

Then he kissed her.

Later, when everyone had gone off to their own rooms, Klaus walked up behind her as she was about to step into the shower.

"Want someone to wash your back?" he asked quietly.

"I don't know. Are you free?"

"No, but I'm reasonable."

"That, husband, is debatable."

"We haven't been in the shower together in a while."

"It's been two days."

"That's about forty-seven hours too long."

"No argument from me."

Klaus kissed her neck. Then he turned her around to face him. "Steam and soap just don't really appeal right now. Maybe later," he said as he picked her up and carried her into the bedroom.

A fire was blazing in the fireplace. A couple of throw pillows were on the floor. Beside them were a wine cooler containing champagne, and two tulip glasses.

"*You've been planning.*"

"*Of course I have. Seducing my beautiful wife is my favorite occupation,*" *he said as he lowered her to the floor and came down to lie on his right side beside her.*

"*And you do it so well,*" *she replied as she touched his face lightly.* "*I love you so much.*"

"*Maybe even as much as I love you.*"

She ran her hand up his leg and stopped when she decided that he was ready, willing, and quite able to finish his plans.

"*Don't stop touching me,*" *he moaned.*

And she didn't. She loved him with her hands and mouth, stroking him, kissing him, taking his penis within her mouth, and teasing it with her tongue. Finally, she straddled him as he lay before the fire and took his penis deep within her before she began to move. His hands were alternately on her breasts and her hips. That part of their lovemaking was brief and intense, but he managed to hold off on his orgasm until she had experienced hers.

Laying together in the firelight, Klaus reached for the champagne and poured them both a glass.

"*No. I don't think I'd better, darling.*"

He looked at her, puzzled. "*Why not?*"

"*It's not good for sprout here,*" *she said as she touched her not quite flat stomach.*

"*Are you sure?*"

"*The test was positive this afternoon. We're going to have another baby in about seven and a half months.*"

Klaus stood and lifted her from the floor. He gently carried her to the bed.

"*I'm not made of glass, husband.*"

"Phase two, just for you. Tonight, you will know that you are loved."

"I know that."

"You will never have any doubts."

"No doubts," Edwina murmured in her sleep as she snuggled deeper into Klaus' arms.

He kissed her forehead. Her eyes came open. "Hi," she said quietly. "I'm glad that you aren't a dream now."

"I'm real, Edwina Elizabeth. But, I can't stay with you much longer tonight."

"I know," she said quietly, only acceptance in her voice. "You have to take care of yourself."

"You are incredible."

"We are incredible," she corrected. She bit her lip. "I have a dream to record. Do you mind?"

"No. Was it a good dream?"

"Yes. Why don't you go get dressed while I record this in my journal?"

He kissed her hard on the mouth once more then got out of bed without further comment. She reached under her pillow and brought out her nightgown, a long fleece dorm shirt. She pulled the garment on over her head.

She got out her dream journal, put on her glasses, and recorded the images from the party and what followed but the faces of the members of the crowd didn't come back to her. She knew that they would haunt her all day until she did remember them.

Klaus' house was familiar to her. She had years of seeing that house. It was just another dream. Or at least that was what she tried to tell herself. Two and one half years of marriage to Klaus, a baby, another on the way, a house full of Christmas guests who all spoke German. But she couldn't shake the images. It was all too real.

Once she had put away the journal, the phone rang. Edwina reached for the phone. No one spoke on the other end. But there was a considerable amount of heavy breathing. She hung up the phone. No sooner had she hung up the phone than it rang again. Same story, heavy breather. At the third call she simply retaliated by turning off the ringer and setting her answering machine to pick up on the first ring, then she shut off the ringer.

"Crank calls?" Klaus asked from the doorway.

"Sounds that way."

"Any suspicions?" he asked as he crossed the room to come to sit beside her on the rumpled bed.

"No proof."

"You think it was your disgruntled tenant?"

"Maybe," she admitted quietly. "Probably."

"I've never seen the point in making crank calls."

"No. That's not your style. If you wanted to harass a woman, you wouldn't limit yourself to pranks like heavy breathing calls. You'd start with something far more direct."

"I'm not sure if that was a compliment or an insult."

"If it were an insult, you'd know it."

"Knowing you, yes, I believe I would. I'm supposed to pick Karen, my sister, up from the airport in about an hour."

"Go, do what you have to do."

He sighed. "I'd rather stay here with you. But a man takes care of all the women in his life."

"As long as the only other women in your life are your sisters, nieces, and eventually maybe our daughters, I'll accept that."

Klaus lightly kissed her forehead. "Does that mean you'll marry me?"

"Probably. There are still things we need to discuss."

"Things? What sort of things?" he asked carefully.

Edwina looked at him. "We don't have time to discuss them right now. You need to get out to the airport and pick up your sister."

"I could send Schmidt."

"You told her that you would pick her up, didn't you?"

"Yes."

"Then you need to pick her up. When you go, take the bodyguards with you."

"No, that I will not do. The guards stay. I will not put you in danger. Leaving you without guards would be placing you in danger. It is not unknown that you have become important to me. I am not without enemies, Edwina," he said.

"Just give me some space, Klaus."

"Talk to me for a few minutes."

"What do you want to talk about?" she asked.

"That hypothetical scientist," he answered in rapid German.

"That is not an interesting subject for conversation," she replied in the same language.

"On the contrary, it is a most interesting subject. This hypothetical scientist, suppose that she were to come against a problem in human genetics to which her work in plant genetics would apply?"

"To augment some trait that is missing or insufficient?"

"Hypothetically."

"Wouldn't it be easier to supplement the diet of this person or to give injections of the missing substance?"

"Perhaps. Suppose that failed."

"Gene therapy might be useful. But it would have to be handled with all possible safeguards."

"Would this hypothetical scientist be interested in taking on a project like that?"

"Is that what you are working on now? Some gene therapy program?"

"Perhaps. The hypothetical scientist might be interested in taking on this hypothetical project."

"Hypothetically, perhaps she might."

"How about in reality?"

"We can talk about this later, sometime when I'm not so tired."

"*Liebling*, you are going to be tired quite a lot from now on. I intend to make love with you regularly. And it will not always be so brief."

She laughed. "Good. Now, good night, Klaus."

"What time will you be out to the house in the morning?"

"My crew chief and I will be there sometime before nine."

"My staff will be anticipating your arrival. My man's name is Kaufmann."

"You won't be there?"

"I'd planned on spending the day dealing with my youngest sister. But I've had business matters arise."

"That's understandable."

"I should let you try to sleep," he said quietly.

"That might be for the best," she said "Come. I need to shut off the fire."

"You're taking this rather well."

"What's not to take well? It was my decision to invite you up and to let things happen between us. And I warned you that it wouldn't be safe for you ever to stay the night with me."

"I was a quite willing participant in case you didn't notice."

She smiled at him. "I *noticed*. Believe me, I noticed."

"Did you now?"

"You are an amazing man who will be late to pick up your sister if you don't get out the door in two minutes."

"I can tell that you are going to be a harsh taskmaster of a wife."

"We'll talk about that later. You need to go now."

"Yes, I do," he told her as he kissed her once more hard.

Edwina followed Klaus downstairs and handed him his overcoat.

"Good night, my dear Edwina. May the angels guard your rest."

"Good night, Klaus."

A few moments later, back in her bedroom, she picked up her rosary and began to try to pray. The chill told her that Catherine had faded in once more.

"Oh, he has a gene therapy program in progress. It's nothing you want to become involved in, Edwina. He's trying to mutate his own genes."

"Go away, Catherine. I'm trying to pray."

"You need to pray only slightly less than you simply need to run from that creature," Catherine said sharply. "Tell him to go away and leave you alone."

"Leave me alone, Catherine."

"You just remember what I've told you about him, and be on your guard."

"Go away, Catherine."

A very sad expression passed over the face of the shade just before the figure faded away.

Edwina went back to her beads. Before she had said even one more prayer, the cats began howling. She threw down her prayer beads and went to see what was bothering them. As near as she could tell after looking through the apartment, the cats had nothing to be excited about. Yet they would not calm down.

Being too wired now to sleep, and not being able to pray with all the noise, she went into the library. She took the coffee tray into the kitchen, warmed the pot of coffee in the microwave, poured it into a thermal carafe, then went to her computer and pulled up her notes on her own research.

After a couple of hours work, she uploaded the files to the remote computer. That was her back up in case anything happened to her main computer. The cats finally settled down about the time that she finished the work.

She stretched out on her bed, picked up her rosary, but was immediately asleep.

Chapter Eight

The alarm clock rang off at the usual time, before dawn. Edwina looked at it in disbelief. It seemed as though she had just gone to sleep. It couldn't be time to get up. But it was. It didn't seem that she should be waking alone but she was.

She forced herself out of bed and into the bathroom for a long hot shower. Wrapping her robe around her, she left the bathroom and stopped by the answering machine to pick up her messages. There were seven messages on the tape. She pressed the "play" key.

The first six were more of the heavy breathing. The next call made her shake. It was clearly Jim Douglass' voice. "Listen, Queen Bitch, I've had it. The poltergeists are destroying my business. I've told you and I've told you. If you won't get rid of the spirits, I will! If the building no longer exists, they can't haunt it. Fire or salt can purify. Fire's easy and cheap. I hope you understand me. I'm not taking any more of this shit. I don't care what I have to do to end it."

Edwina quickly ejected the full size cassette tape and labeled it. She put a fresh tape into the answering machine. Then she turned back on the ringer.

She dialed her uncle's home number.

Uncle Lawrence answered it. "Lawrence Greene."

"Uncle? It's Edwina."

"What's the matter, Edwina? You sound upset."

"I'd been getting crank phone calls, so I shut off the ringer and left the answering machine to get it. My tenant was unwise enough to call and leave a threatening message on tape."

"You have the tape?"

"I do. What do you want me to do with it?"

"Call the police, Edwina. Report the threat. Tell them that it was left on your phone answering machine and that you have the tape. I'll be by with the paperwork on the psychiatric complaint. You *will* sign it. We have to get this man off the street before he harms himself or someone else. Even making a threat of doing something like this shows him to be profoundly unstable."

She sighed. "Don't tell Grandmother about this."

"Your grandmother has eyes in back of her head. Nothing passes under her radar."

"Tell me about it."

"Will you sign the complaint and get this man some much needed help?"

"Yes. But I've got an early appointment to walk off a landscape contract. I won't be back at the shop until about ten thirty."

"Stop by my office on the way back to your shop, then. The papers will be at the front desk. Sign them. I'll get them filed by noon. But call the police now, Edwina."

"Yes, Uncle."

Knowing there was a chance she might see Klaus, Edwina didn't want to wear jeans. There was always a gleam in his eye when he saw her legs. But she'd be working. So she compromised between work clothes and nicer clothes, settling for the nicer of her work clothes. She put on a softly faded denim skirt, a blue version of the black one she had worn the other night. With it, she pulled on a navy blue turtleneck sweater and her black leather western boots. Over everything, she decided that she would wear her black leather jacket. It wasn't particularly pretty, but it was better than jeans and a cotton flannel shirt.

The patrolmen came within a half-hour of Edwina's call. She didn't like doing this, calling the police had thrown off her entire morning schedule. She wouldn't be able to make Mass. At this rate, she knew that she would be lucky to be able to get out to Klaus' house in time to get the work done there and get back to the shop by the official opening time.

Edwina told the officers everything about Jim, including his attack on her the day before. She showed them the bruise where Jim had taken hold of her.

"Why didn't you call us yesterday?" one officer demanded.

"I thought I could handle this. Now I realize that the man is totally beyond reasoning with. He is dangerous, to himself and to everyone around him. And it's way beyond anything I can handle. He's not sane. Unless he gets help he's going to hurt someone or himself. I no longer stand convinced that he was attacked early Sunday morning. I think he set that up."

One of the officers nodded. "Could we listen to this tape?"

"Of course," Edwina said as she popped the tape into a player she kept under the counter.

Jim's words came flooding over the speakers. Edwina shuddered hearing them again.

At the end of the tape, she shut off the player and ejected the tape. Then she handed it to the officers. "You'll need this as evidence. I want him stopped before he burns the building down. There's already been one small fire."

"We'll do our best," one of the patrolmen said.

"Will that be good enough?"

The older of the two patrolmen sighed. "We can only try."

"Then I can hope that it will be enough," she said as she looked at her watch. "Are we done here? I have a business appointment with a client."

"Yes. A detective will probably be in contact with you."

Edwina handed them her card. "This has my cell number on it. If I'm not here, I can be reached there."

She sighed as the police officers left. She hadn't wanted to do this. But Jim had left her no choice.

Her crew chief and partner in the nursery, Jennifer, came into the shop just after the police had left. "What were the cops here for, Ed?"

With a shake of her head, Edwina said, "It doesn't matter. They'll handle it. I need about ten minutes to talk with people before we go out to Doctor von Bruner's home. I'll be right back. We have work to do there."

"I brought the nursery pick-up. It's parked down the block. Come when you are done."

Edwina talked to each of her remaining tenants, briefly filling them in on the situation. She figured she owed them a warning about Jim.

* * * * *

Klaus lived in a gated community. Edwina gave her name to the security guard and they were let through with no problem.

Edwina looked at the house and wanted to run as Jennifer parked the pick up in the driveway. She'd seen this house before, in her dreams, for the last fifteen years. It was a Norman style white stone house, with twin turrets flanking the entry foyer.She knew without seeing it, what the house would be like inside. She knew the layout, the colors, everything.

"This is some house Ed," Jennifer said quietly.

Edwina sighed. "Yeah. But we've got work to do. Come on. The job is in the back yard."

"You don't even want to see the inside?"

"No. Let's get to work."

"Whatever you say," the other woman said quietly. "But, don't you think that you'd better let the staff know that we are here just so that they don't call the cops?"

"I'm sure that the gate house has informed them that we were on our way."

Jennifer shook her head. "What's bothering you Ed?"

"Jennifer, you wouldn't believe me if I told you. Now let's get the job done. I've got a very long day ahead of me and a big party tonight for my grandmother."

"Stress makes you crabby, you know that Ed?"

"You have no idea Jennifer," she replied dryly. "Come on. Daylight's wasting."

Klaus looked at the image on the security monitor as he spoke on the telephone. Edwina was here. He had expected her. But she didn't look happy.

Finishing his business call, he dialed his sister, Karen's, bedroom extension. "Go outside and spend some of that excessive energy of yours on your horse."

Karen laughed sleepily. "Klaus, this is just further evidence that big brothers should be drowned at birth. Or in your case, smothered in garlic," she teased.

"Karen, please do as you are asked."

Then, in her first serious tone of the day, she asked, "Why do you want me to go out riding at this hour of the morning? Who's outside that I'm supposed to see?"

"Your future sister-in-law, Edwina Johnson."

"The botanist/geneticist?"

"The same."

"Does she know about your marital plans for her, brother dear?"

"Yes and she's running scared."

"If she is running scared, why is she here?"

"I've employed her to redesign the back garden."

"That's interesting. Is this work she does regularly?"

"Ever since she walked away from her last employer she's been trying to launch a business venture of her own. I suspect it is a cover story for her to use to hide behind while her research continues. The job gives me an excuse to see her."

"Since when do you need an excuse for pursuing a woman?"

"Just go outside Brat and be your charming self. Let her know that I have redeeming features."

"Do you have redeeming features?" Karen teased unmercifully. "I've never noticed any."

"Karen, how many favors do I beg of you?"

"Very few, Klaus," she admitted.

"I am begging you now. Quickly throw on your riding habit and boots, and go down to the stables. On your way, introduce yourself to her. She speaks very good German. Be that charming self that you show all of your friends, and not the wicked-tongued brat that you are to family. I want her charmed, not frightened off."

"This woman is important—that important—to you?"

"She will be my wife, Karen. And she has the best chance of anyone of coming up with a cure for this cursed condition of mine. You've seen her research. I would say that makes her doubly important to me."

Klaus' sister sighed. "Very well, my dear brother. It will take me a few moments to get presentable. After all, you did pick me up at the airport quite late last night or early this morning, rather."

"Don't waste any time."

"Klaus, there are times that your disability is quite wearying."

"You don't have to live inside it. I do."

"I know, my dear," she said compassionately. "Does she know?"

Klaus sighed. "No, not yet. Not completely. She's deduced part of it. But, I haven't had the courage to tell her all of it."

"Don't you think that you had better tell her? Especially, as you are obviously planning for her to help you solve it."

"Her assistance is hers to give or to withhold. I wouldn't dream of coercing her one way or another. I love her, Karen. I can live—reasonably well—this way for the rest of my life. But I don't think I could live well at all without her in my life from now on. I do not want to scare her away from me."

"You should be totally honest with her, then, Klaus. She has a right to know what she is getting into as she becomes involved with you."

"She's laying out the new garden. I expect that she will be here another twenty five to thirty minutes, Karen."

"Okay. I'm going."

"Thank you."

"Shall I bring her in to you?"

"No. I told her I was to be occupied with business matters today."

She sighed. "You will have to tell her, Klaus. Sooner or later."

"I would rather it be later than sooner."

His sister sighed once more. "It is your life, Brother. However, you are making a mistake of the first order. She's bound to feel a degree of betrayal that you haven't trusted her."

"Just go on out and talk with her, please," he said before he hung up the phone and sat back in his dimly lit office, looking at the monitors from the outside cameras. There were times that he really hated the restrictions of his condition.

Seven minutes later, he saw Karen, dressed in her riding habit, walk out into the back lawn.

Edwina and the other woman were taking measurements.

Klaus wished that he could hear what they were saying. But there were only cameras not microphones on the security system.

Karen walked up to Edwina. "*Guten morgen.*"

Edwina looked at her. "*Guten morgen,*" she replied cautiously.

"My brother told me that you would be here this morning. I am Karen von Bruner," Karen said in rapid German.

Edwina answered in German, "You are Klaus' youngest sister."

"Ah, then, he's told you about me."

"Should he not have?"

Karen laughed softly. "What did he tell you about me?"

"Just that you were spending your birthday with friends in Geneva, instead of at the Opera with him. How was Geneva?"

"Much as it always is."

"And the young man whom you went to see?"

The younger woman blushed slightly. "Also much as he always is."

"Is your brother here?"

"*Ja.* He's in his office. He's busy with his phone conferences. Seems that he spends most of every day tied up with business. He's driven. What he needs is someone like you to give him something besides business to think about. He needs a woman who will challenge him. Having read your dissertations it's clear that you can keep up with him."

Edwina felt her face grow warm. "Right now, I need to finish this work so that I can get back to my own business."

"Can you come to dinner tonight. We can talk more then."

"No, I'm sorry. I have family obligations tonight. It's my grandmother's birthday. There's a party at her club in her honor."

Karen sighed. "I understand that. Family is important."

"You were on your way to the stables from your dress."

"Do you ride?"

"Yes. I've always liked horses."

"You are welcome to come out here any time and use any of the horses."

"That's kind of you."

"No, it's rather selfish, if you must know the truth. Even with the exercise boys, the animals do not get the amount of work they need. And Klaus only has time to ride at night. I'd like to get to know you better."

"That would be nice. I think I'd enjoy that."

"I'll leave you to your work. It's nice to meet you, Edwina."

"Nice to meet you, too, Karen."

"My brother is not an easy man. However, he's well worth the effort. He can be quite charming when he sets his mind to it."

"I had noticed that. He can also be quite intimidating. Of course, it would never do to let him know just how intimidating he appears."

"An understatement of purely British proportions. He has a big enough head as it is," Karen agreed, still speaking German. "He's just so perfect at everything he puts his hand to. I've always been envious of him. Everything has always seemed to come so easy for him. It wasn't until the last few years I've understood just how hard he works and how seriously he takes his obligations."

"Whether those obligations are real or imagined," Edwina added quietly.

Klaus' sister laughed boldly. Then she spoke in English, "I like you, Edwina. It will be good to have you for a sister-in-law."

"Don't rush me."

Karen's eyes sparkled with humor. "Oh, I'd imagine that my brother is doing a good enough job of that all by himself. Has he proposed yet?"

"Is that a common practice with him?"

Karen laughed. "Of course not. I've never known him to let any woman get under his skin the way that he has with you. He's utterly besotted."

"Don't tell him, but I think it's very mutual."

"Yes. You will be very good for him."

"It's a wise sister who knows her brother."

Karen just smiled. "I'll let you get to work now."

Jennifer looked at Edwina after Karen walked away. "I didn't know that you were seeing the guy who lives here."

"No reason that you should have known."

"Are you going to marry him?"

"I'm not quite certain. Probably."

"Is he as filthy rich as this place would indicate?"

"I really wouldn't know. Money hasn't been a serious discussion with us. Now can we get back to work?"

"You know that we're on candid camera?" Jennifer asked. "Security cameras have been monitoring us from the moment that we stepped foot on the place."

"I am aware of that," Edwina replied. "But we still have work to do. So let's get to it, Jen. Okay? The sooner we get done the sooner we can get back to the shop and get the plans drawn. I pretty well know what is going in here but I need measurements and soil samples to be sure."

"You're the boss."

"No," Edwina said as she nodded towards the house, "he's the boss. We both just work for him."

When Edwina was nearly done with the measurements, Klaus' butler, Kaufman, came out to speak to her. "*Herr* Baron von Bruner would like to speak with you, *Fraulein* Doctor."

"You go back to the nursery Jen. I'll get back to town later."

Jennifer smiled at her friend. "Okay. If you're sure."

"I'm sure."

"*Fraulein* Doctor?"

"*Ja*, Kaufman. I am coming."

Chapter Nine

Edwina hadn't wanted to face the fact that her dreams had revealed this house with such accuracy. She knew the full layout of the building.

"*Fraulein*," Kaufman said quietly. "Herr Baron is in his office. If you would walk this way."

"I know the way, Kaufman, thank you. You may return to your regular duties."

Kaufman looked at her in disbelief. "*Fraulein*?"

She smiled and gave him directions to Klaus' office. "I do know where I am going Kaufman. You may return to your regular duties."

Edwina made her way to his office without assistance. Klaus was watching on the monitors. She didn't bother knocking. She simply walked in, closed the door behind her, and sat down.

"You summoned me?"

Klaus smiled at her. "I asked you to come see me."

"What's on your mind?"

"What do you think about the garden?"

"I feel guilty taking your money. This is going to be fun."

Klaus rose from his desk and walked over to her. He pulled her to her feet and into his arms. "Surely you didn't think I asked you here for the sake of talking business?"

"Whatever else I am, I am not naïve, Klaus."

"You are in a strange mood, Edwina."

"It's been a strange morning so far."

"In what way, Edwina?"

"What? Your watchdogs didn't tell you?" she demanded with a hint of bitterness in her voice. She heard that attitude in her voice and was ashamed. Klaus had shown her nothing but kindness and gentleness, along with the passion of his soul. He didn't deserve her taking her bad mood out on him.

"The bodyguards are there to protect you not to report to me about your comings and goings. What do you think I should have known?"

Edwina sighed. "Jim, my paint store tenant, left a threatening message on my machine this morning."

"What kind of threat?"

"He says that he will burn the building."

"That man needs serious help."

"I'm swearing out a complaint to get him taken in for a psychiatric evaluation."

"That sounds prudent."

"Yeah that's me, Miss Prudence," Edwina said dryly.

Klaus looked at her questioningly. "Prudence is often a good thing."

"It's a safe thing. Whether it's good or not depends on the risks one foregoes and on one's comfort level for midnight regrets for sins of omission. Of course I don't believe them to be any worse than regrets for sins of commission."

"Edwina?" Klaus asked carefully. "Are you trying to tell me something?"

"Just be quiet and hold me, Klaus. I need the comfort of your arms."

"My arms are yours whenever you want them."

"I've never been comfortable leaning on others," she said quietly. "I could become too dependent on you Klaus."

"A woman can never be too dependent on a man who loves her."

One corner of Edwina's mouth twitched upwards in a parody of a smile. "And when that love dies?"

"My love for you will never die. Don't worry about that."

"How can you be so certain Klaus? I know very few people who have managed to have happy marriages."

"We will. We both take the idea of marriage seriously."

"I wish I could be that confident."

"Anytime you want to walk away from me, just say the word, Edwina. I will not force my presence on you."

"I've got to get back to town shortly. The shop won't open without me there. But that doesn't mean I wouldn't rather be here with you, Klaus."

"I know. I'd love to take you upstairs to my bedroom and keep you there the rest of the day, tomorrow, the rest of the week, as long as I could get by with keeping you here until people came looking for you. Yet we both have obligations. I've got a teleconference in just under an hour and I'll be tied up most of the rest of the day with other conferences."

"Sometimes I'd love to be able to just play hooky."

"Play hooky?"

"That's an Americanism, Klaus. It means to leave one's obligations untended in favor of going off to do other more pleasurable things."

"What would give you pleasure?"

Edwina smiled at him. "I can think of a number of things."

"Can you? My list may be longer than yours."

"Maybe. Mine begins by taking your clothes off of you and spending the rest of the day in your bed making love," Edwina offered.

"Hmmm… Well, our lists are similar in that respect."

"I suppose I had better be leaving you. You probably have a good deal of work to do."

"Don't go yet. There are some things I need to show to you."

"Then show them to me. I sent Jen back alone. So I'm at your mercy. Can you free Schmidt or someone to drive me back to town?"

"I'm sure Hans is out there. He'll drive you back to town. If he's not there I'll free Schmidt to drive you."

"I could phone for a taxi."

"Nonsense. Can you spare about a half hour?"

She looked at her watch. "Not much more than that."

"Come with me. There are things I want you to see while you are here."

Klaus led her to his personal lab. He opened a file cabinet and removed a large envelope. Out of the envelope, he brought five DNA test strips. He hung those on the glass and turned on the light behind the glass so that she could easily read them.

Edwina looked at the strips for a long time. "I've never seen anything like it. What species is this describing?"

"*Liebling*, that's my DNA."

She looked at him, then at the strips, then back at him. "It can't be. There's only a four percent change in the DNA from ape to man," she said pointedly. "There has to be at least a ten percent differential between this and normal human DNA."

Klaus nodded. "There is eleven percent. And it is my DNA."

She turned her eyes back to the strips, trying hard to keep this in perspective. "You are certain that the tests were done correctly?"

"They were done correctly. I've had the tests run every year for thirty years, Edwina. The results are always the same. The technology has improved. But the results remain consistent. What you have up there are the last five years' tests."

"Well this," she said pointing at an area of the strip with a laser pointer she picked up, "is not entirely unexpected. Neither is this. This area is another matter, entirely. I've never seen anything like this."

"I don't imagine that you have. There are only two rare medical conditions we've been able to identify that have similar DNA."

"Yours and what other?"

"Lycanthropy," he said quietly.

Her head jerked around suddenly to look at him. "What did you say?" she demanded harshly.

"You heard me quite well, Edwina."

"Lycanthropy is a rare mental illness characterized by delusions of transformations into wolves or other dangerous animals, acute anxiety, obsession with cemeteries and forests, preoccupation with religious phenomenology — particularly with a sense of being cursed, and an expression of sexual and aggressive urges centering on bestiality. It often correlates with profound schizophrenia," Edwina replied, her voice more sharp than she had intended. "People who believe they are were-animals are insane. No one can become a wolf. Life just doesn't work that way."

Klaus smiled then quoted from Shakespeare, "'There are more things in heaven and earth, Horatio, than are dreamt of in your philosophy.'"

"And what has Hamlet to do with this discussion?"

"Watch, carefully, my beloved, learn without fear. Know that I would never, in any form, harm you or allow any harm to come to you. Above everything trust me, Edwina, I beg of you."

He stepped back from her several paces.

Edwina watched in growing horror as Klaus morphed into a large wolf. She wanted to scream, but the sound would not come from her throat. His clothes were loosely around the form of the wolf. The wolf walked to her, as he did, he walked out of Klaus' clothes leaving them lay on the floor behind him.

Then the wolf stuck his nose under her skirt and began to lick her knees. His licks went higher up her leg until he was nuzzling and licking at her panties. She stepped backwards into the wall. The animal followed her.

The wolf stood on its hind legs and placed its front paws on her shoulders. It began to lick her face and neck.

Edwina forced herself to take a deep breath. This was Klaus. As hard as that was to believe, *this was Klaus*. This fur-covered mass of muscle laving her face was the man she loved. It didn't make sense, but she couldn't deny the evidence of her own eyes. This utterly boggled her mind. This was completely beyond everything that she knew. There were only two options. She could go into denial— fight the evidence of her own senses—or she could deal with this. He'd asked her to trust him. She let out that deep breath in a slow stream and imagined the stress and tension leaving her body as she exhaled.

Then she started to laugh because Klaus' wolf-tongue tickled as it danced across the sensitive skin of her throat. Lifting her hand, she began to rub the wolf behind his ears. "Okay, that's enough already. I took a bath this morning. I don't need another," she teased. "You make a gorgeous wolf, but you are a more handsome man. You want to come back to me now?"

Just as suddenly as the wolf had appeared, the wolf was gone. A naked Klaus stood before her. "Oh no, it's not enough, Edwina. It has barely begun. You scratched behind my ears and now I'll follow you anywhere," he said with a teasing glint in his eye.

"The only place I want you to follow me is into ecstasy."

"*Liebling*, that can be easily arranged."

"There's not time this morning."

"There's always time," he countered as just before he kissed her hard. His hands went beneath her skirt and tugged down her panties. They fell to her ankles. "Haven't we had this conversation before? Time is nearly irrelevant."

She stepped out of her panties. "I can almost believe that."

"*'Come live with me and be my love and we will all the pleasures prove,'*" he said, quoting Christopher Marlowe's poem, as he lifted her skirt and kneed her legs apart.

"*'Love is not love that alters when it alteration finds,'*" she answered with a line from one of Shakespeare's sonnets as she wrapped her arms around his neck and held on tightly.

His hands went to her thighs and lifted her legs up around his hips. Without another word, he drove his hard length into her.

She moaned raggedly as he stretched and filled her. There was only time to feel, not to think. Sensations overwhelmed her. Very shortly, she found herself on the brink of release. What was it with this man that he could give her so much satisfaction?

Edwina cried out a few moments later as she climaxed and the world around her went dark.

When she came back to herself, she was sitting on Klaus' lap, on the floor of his lab. He was still naked.

"I take it you found pleasure?" he teased her.

She kissed his cheek. "You know I did. Did you?"

"*Frau !* I could never fail to take pleasure in you."

"Get dressed," she said as she stood. "We need to talk." She reached down and pulled on her panties.

He nodded. Then he morphed into a mass of vapor which floated over to the empty clothes on the floor. The garments filled up, and then Klaus was back. He rose to his feet.

She looked at him for a long moment. Then she swallowed hard, "That was...er...some trick... Klaus. "

He nodded. "I know that this all must be difficult for you to accept. You are doing much better with it than I had expected you to."

She looked back at the DNA strip because she didn't feel able to look at him. "I've never seen anything like this. I'm still not sure I believe it, although I have seen it."

"Believe it. I find that it is advisable to shift into forms that are about the same mass and density. But other forms—like that wolf and the cloud I just did—are quite possible. They're just much more difficult."

"But in spite of the fact that you morphed into a wolf, lycanthropy is not your condition. You said that there were two conditions with the same DNA pattern—your condition and lycanthropy," she said thinking aloud, her voice shaking.

"That is correct. I am not a lycanthrope."

She looked back at the DNA strip. She sighed heavily as she tried to absorb this revelation and sort out what it means. "Yes. Perhaps that would fit what I'm seeing here. And this area here," she said pointing at another spot on the DNA report. "This is beyond merely interesting."

"I thought you'd see that."

"Just how old are you, Klaus?"

He sighed. "I brought you here to see this. I thought you ought to know the full truth about the man you are considering marrying."

"How old are you, Klaus?" she demanded once more.

"The man you see before you was born forty-one years ago."

"That isn't what I asked," Edwina replied sharply. "How old are *you*, not the form you appear to have, *you*?"

Klaus sighed. Then he spoke with patience and pride mingling in his voice, "Very good, Edwina. You do think outside conventions extremely effectively. I hoped that you would see this and understand. Ways of reckoning time, and the importance of doing so, have changed substantially over the course of my life to date, making an accurate number for my age difficult to determine. I am one thousand, six hundred, and twenty-seven years old, Edwina, at least that's the best approximate reckoning of my age that I've been able to make."

She sat down on a nearby stool and looked at him as she tried to think this out. "One thousand…" she echoed on a disbelieving breath. "How in the…" She shook her head as if to clear it. "Your sisters, are they…?"

"The girls are normal humans. I took this form when Klaus was a toddler just as I've taken the forms of other young men in my family over the centuries in order to continue living among people. My sisters don't know this part of it. They are my people. We are just more distantly related than they believe. I adopted them as sisters when they were born. In every way that counts they are my sisters. And I love them dearly."

"So why tell me this now?"

"Because I love you and I want you to know the full truth about me. There must be no further secrets between us, Edwina, none at all. I do not want you looking at me in horror one morning after we've been married for thirty years as the full truth dawns on you."

She looked at him for a long moment. "That's happened to you."

"Yes."

"I'm sorry for the pain that caused you."

"It was a long time ago."

"What is the full truth Klaus? How many other shocks do you have in store for me?"

"Look at the DNA, Edwina. God gifted you with an exceptional mind. Use it. Everything about my physical life is encoded there on that strip."

"What happened to the original Klaus, the one whose form you took?"

"He died."

"Did you kill him?" She hated to ask that question, yet she couldn't help herself. She needed to know exactly what kind of man this was standing before her.

"No. He died from a fever. The body was given a Christian burial and I took his form."

"That's convenient. Who did they think they were burying?"

"My former form, the grandfather of the family. I was able to change the child's appearance to conform to that of my former form. I'd had that form for almost ninety years. It was time to move on."

She sighed. "This is all quite a lot to digest. And I don't even want to know how you could replace an old version of yourself for a younger one."

"Yes, I understand. It is a great deal for now. I strongly debated about telling you any of this. But I wanted you to know."

"Again, why?"

"This is the third time I have told you the answer. I don't want any secrets between us," Klaus said patiently. "Your decision to be in my life has to be free, conscious and informed. I could easily bend your will to mine. Yet I want you to maintain your free will and make your own choices. To do that you have to know everything."

"You said the abnormalities were acquired. How were they acquired?"

Klaus sighed. "There is only one way, Edwina, to acquire this condition that is through a subject mixing blood with someone who has the abnormalities. Near as we can tell the exchanged blood acts as a reprogramming agent for the subject's DNA. We've been trying to understand the reprogramming mechanism for many years. The science is just about to the place where we are beginning to get our first glance at the real nature of the process."

"Reprogramming? Like a retrovirus?"

"As near as we can tell, it seems to be a retrovirus that causes this condition."

"Understanding and duplicating that mechanism could be the key to curing a number of diseases," she thought aloud.

"Yes. It could be. Also, we might eventually be able to reprogram our DNA to allow us to walk freely in the sunlight and thus improve our quality of life."

"There is that," she allowed.

"I know that you haven't been prepared for this, Edwina. And that it has to be a shock to you."

"You've talked to me about having children. What would the chances be of this being passed on to them?"

"There is no chance of that. The genetic condition is filtered out in the production of egg and sperm. My children, even children by women who have these same abnormalities, have always been fully human. There is no sex linkage between my condition and future offspring."

She rubbed her neck in hopes that could dispel the threatening tension headache and she looked at him. "So it's an organ specific retrovirus," she observed. "Hmmm...That's interesting."

"As nearly as we can determine, yes, that would be a good description of the situation."

"How many children have you had, Klaus?"

"Five hundred and eighty seven that I know are mine. None of them are now living. Most of the lines of their descendants have died out."

"There remain other people like you? You are not the last of your kind on earth I take it?"

"You take it correctly. There are others, men and women, in every nation on the face of the earth. There are also many other persons with lycanthropy. They — at least — have the saving grace of being able to walk in the daylight, although they do not have the immune system modification my people have and they do not live beyond a normal mortal span. Legends about people of my kind have sprung up in every country — similar legends with different names and gross distortions about who and what we are. It's in the folklore. It's in popular horror literature. It's even made it to children's television programming and sunglass advertisements."

"What are you?"

"I am only a man who loves you Edwina. That is the only important thing I am. Everything else fades into insignificance."

She looked at him for a very long time as she forced herself to put aside preconceived ideas about reality and deal with the data before her. "Vampire. You are what is known in legend as a vampire," she said on a breath as everything kicked into place in her mind. The idea was absolutely unbelievable. Yet that was the only answer fitting the data before her.

Klaus nodded and smiled. "I knew that you could come to the correct conclusion Edwina if given the access to the evidence. Your reputation for thinking outside of conventions is well deserved," he answered with a mixture of pride and satisfaction in his voice.

"You don't spontaneously combust in sunlight."

"No. However, UV radiation is extremely harmful. With a long enough exposure to the sun any of my kind would die."

"What is long enough exposure?"

"That's debatable. We try to avoid all UV because we just don't know. But sometimes we need to go out during the day. That's why we developed high level sun-block lotions, UV filters in contact lenses, and a relatively new line of UV shielding clothing. We do everything possible to shield ourselves from harmful effects."

"You don't hunt people and kill them for their blood."

He sighed heavily. "That much of the legends at least has some basis in fact. There was a time when my kind did prey upon normals. I've never taken enough blood from anyone to kill them. I know people of my kind who have done that. We—the council—have made them pay the price for their murdering ways. It's been over a thousand years since I've gone hunting for blood at all. Most of us discovered that it wasn't at all necessary to hunt."

"Why is it not necessary?"

"We learned to take what we need from a sexual partner during intimacy while distracting them with pleasure and no one was the wiser. There was a degree of lassitude in our partners afterwards, but they easily recovered. It was no worse than the lightheadedness some people get when leaving a blood bank after donating a unit of blood. We never take more than that."

She looked at him for a long time without saying anything. "Have you fed from me?" she finally asked. "Klaus, did you take blood from me last night or just a few moments ago?"

"No, Edwina Elizabeth, I did not. There was a moment I was tempted to do so. But I did not. I wanted to love you, not to use you. I haven't taken blood directly from a person in almost forty years. These days, I simply channel units off of blood banks. We have found that we can take the units that they would destroy for being out of date and use those. The corporation takes them for 'research purposes.' We still get the benefits and there is no potential for harming anyone. It is not the same but it works. Like the difference between picking an apple off the tree and eating canned applesauce, it is not the same experience."

"Most of you have given up hunting, you said."

"There are still a few who fail to conform to the international conventions. When we find them we stop them."

"How?"

"We handle it legally, according the laws of the council and the rules of the international conventions. Three convictions for hunting means that the community imposes capital punishment. We have to live in peace with other people. We can't have the hysteria that once gave rise to mobs of vampire hunters. No one wants a war. We may be stronger and faster than normal humans but humans outnumber us greatly. We are content to coexist peacefully, preferably with a human population who is mostly content to think of us as tales from folklore and the mentally ill."

"Three convictions in what time frame?"

"There is no time frame."

"For a race that is virtually immortal that is rather steep punishment."

"It is not as draconian as the former law that allowed summary execution of anyone found hunting."

"With the talk of executions, you can die other than from a stake to the heart or sunlight I presume."

"We can die from a good many causes. We have a tremendous immune system that fights off every disease that we've ever come across. We heal comparatively quickly from most injuries. But we can die from any trauma that would kill any other person, as well as from exposure to UV radiation. And we are no more mentally stable than any other population, so we have our shares of serious depressions and resultant suicides."

Edwina sighed. "I see."

"Do you?"

"Klaus... Is that really your name?"

"Close enough. My original name was an earlier version of this name."

"Klaus, this exchange of blood that makes one a vampire is it usually done during sex?"

He looked at her for a long time. "It can be. It usually is, as it is less traumatic when the transition is cloaked in a sensual haze."

"Transition. Yes. That was the word you used in my dream."

"What have you dreamt, Edwina?"

She told him of her dream.

"I see," he said quietly. "I have run across very few souls with your gift for seeing."

"I'm not so sure that it is always a gift Klaus. Have you the ability to interfere in dreams?"

His eyes grew hard for a brief moment, and she knew that she had angered him. "No. None of my kind has that ability. We can influence waking thought, make people forget things they've witnessed or experienced, and substitute other memories for those things we wish to be forgotten, but we can not influence dreams. That sort of thing is done only by spirit entities like your resident ghost."

"I'm feeling my way here, Klaus. This all is so like fantasy. In the last few months, I've had to come to terms with the reality of all manner of what would be called the paranormal — spirits, and now werewolves and vampires."

He nodded. "It is difficult to adopt a different way of thinking about reality. Yet, you are doing quite well with it. I admire your resiliency."

She blew a large stream of air out between her teeth. "I'm still processing all of this."

"And you will be for some time. I've given you much to think about."

"You say that you want me to make a conscious, free and informed choice. That sounds all well and good. But I do not know any others of your kind."

"How do you know that? We don't wear red fangs on our lapels declaring our status."

She was silent for a moment. "There was a professor while I was doing my doctoral work who only taught at night. He was allergic to sunlight."

"Carl Roddenberg."

"Yes. Roddenberg. Is he one of your people?"

"I've known Carl for well over a hundred years. He's a good man."

Edwina sighed. "This is getting even stranger by the moment."

"I'd imagine that it seems that way."

"Immortality."

"Not quite. We are quite mortal but our life span is long. We don't age."

"This longevity comes with a price. Never to be able to lie out on a beach during the day and feel the sun."

"That's not particularly healthy for anyone."

"Not to be able to work in a garden by daylight."

"There is that."

"Not to be able to run and play outdoors with one's children during the day."

"That's the hardest part of this state of life. Watching one's children grow up and being unable to share their lives fully with them, knowing that you will watch them die in what is a truly short time."

"The other side of this question of immortality is to be able to carry out one's work to its logical extension. To be able to continue to make progress with one's research, to make a real difference—that is tempting."

"There is a downside to that as well in that you always have to read and stay current, have to relearn, unlearn, and learn fresh new things. Having to change form every eighty to one hundred years so that people don't grow overly suspicious about you, is challenging. It is hard to be an adult in a child's body."

"I can't begin to understand how that feels," she admitted.

"Think about this fully, Edwina. Once that barrier between your state of life and mine is crossed, there is no way—at the moment—of going back. Aging as you know it stops."

"But you do age?"

"Not as you understand it. We have no decay, no arthritis, no diseases, no wear and tear. But the years do come to sit heavily upon some of us. We live in time yet outside of time."

"Stupid question."

"There is no such thing. I'll tell you anything that you want to know."

She sighed. "Do you have fangs?"

Klaus smiled at her as he did, his canines lengthened. Then they shortened. "It's something we control as an aspect of changing form. At one time, the fangs were a tool for acquiring the blood we need to survive. Now, they are something like human wisdom teeth — something that we are evolving away from."

"Will you show me your original form?"

"If you would like, Edwina. It truly isn't that much different from this one."

She watched as he slightly, ever so slightly, changed appearance. He shrank several inches in height and broadened out more through the chest and shoulders. Even then, he was a handsome man.

"Thank you."

He changed back to the form that she knew him as possessing. "Have you any further questions?"

"You understand that I need to think about this."

"I understand. I've given you a great deal to think about. Just know that I love you, Edwina. I will love you whether you decide to marry me or not or whether you decide to transition to my state or not. Those decisions are independent of one another. All I ask is that you do not discuss this with people. I have not broken rules by talking to you about it, however doing so is profoundly discouraged. If you choose not to transition, I will have to remove the memory of this conversation from you. It is easier if I do not have to chase down others to whom you may have talked and look into their minds, then scrub them of this knowledge as well. If you need someone to talk to, I can arrange for you to speak with my chaplain. He knows everything."

"Is he another of your kind?"

Klaus smiled broadly. "Your mind is a treasure, Edwina. Yes, Fr. Sebastien is one of my kind as you so delicately put it."

"I understand the restriction on speaking to others. That is a sensible precaution for the safety of everyone." Edwina lightly kissed his cheek. "Thank you for being honest with me."

"How could I be otherwise? I love you."

"Oh, Klaus!" she said quietly. "I'm trying to think of this as your simply belonging to another race or nationality. This is hard to get my mind around. Your DNA means that you are the equivalent of a different species from me. I am more different from you than an ape in a zoo is from me. It feels odd."

He nodded. "I understand. But, don't think about it that way."

"Don't some of your people think of it that way?"

He sighed heavily. "There are some in the community who tend to look down on normal humans," he admitted.

"Or to look at us as just a source for nutrition, companionship, and sexual satisfaction, much like a cross between a cow, a dog, and a whore?"

He was visibly taken aback by that comment. "There are times that you see too much," he admitted reluctantly.

"The legends about holy water, crosses, and other Catholic items being harmful to your kind are just legends?"

"Since we were made to be evil in legend, it was only logical to make good things antithetical to us in legend."

"All vampires are not Catholic?"

"No. We're a pretty diverse lot, just the normal population. You will find Catholics, Protestants, Buddhists, Hindis, Moslems, Atheists, you name it, among us. There is one religious order in the Church that draws its members primarily from my group. They live their lives in silence, darkness, and prayer when cloistered. When outside of the cloister, they generally are under the protection of another of my kind."

"What about garlic?"

"A blood thinner. It's not lethal, but we tend to avoid lots of it. A little never hurts."

"Do newly transitioned vampires get cautioned not to play with their food?"

"Edwina, you are becoming hysterical," he warned quietly.

"No, I passed hysterical some time ago," she told him in an all too controlled voice. "I'm trying to hold it together. I really am. I need to think about this Klaus. I feel betrayed. I fell in love with you. But you aren't the man I believed you to be."

"I am the same man, Edwina. I think you've known all along who and what I am. The problem is that you haven't had to realize that you knew it."

She closed her eyes. "You may be right," she admitted. "I have to have time to think this out."

"Take what time you need. I want you to be absolutely certain."

She touched his face. "Odd feeling or not, betrayal or not, I still want you, Klaus."

He turned his head and kissed her palm. "I will always love and cherish you, Edwina."

"Like you loved and cherished all those who came before me?"

"No. There was only the one who I longed for as a life partner before you. I made the mistake of transitioning her—converting her, if you will be more comfortable with that term—without giving her a choice into my state of life because I wanted her with me so desperately."

"What happened to her?"

"She killed herself. I don't think I will ever forgive myself for my role in her unhappiness," Klaus said quietly, painfully as he looked beyond her. "She was never able to settle into her new state. She—like you—was a morning person, and the deprivation of the ability to be in the sun saddened her beyond words. The woman I loved hated me in the end, and died with curses for me upon her lips."

Then he looked at her, making eye contact. Her heart melted at the pain she saw in his eyes.

"Oh, Klaus," she said quietly, sympathetically, as she took him in her arms and held him. "I wish I could stay here now. I need to go by my uncle's office and swear out that complaint against Jim. Only then can Uncle get the process begun. And I've got a shop to open."

Klaus stepped back from her. "Hans will drive you. But first would you like to see the rest of my house?"

"I've seen most of the house in my dreams over the years. I'd like to spend more time with you. But, you've got a teleconference and I've got to return to town."

"Come on, at least meet my chaplain. You'll like Father Sabastien."

Klaus wasn't wrong. Edwina immediately found herself liking the white haired gentleman who was Klaus' chaplain.

Chapter Ten

The Monday night birthday party for her grandmother was well underway at the country club where her grandmother had been an active member for sixty-five years. It wasn't every day that the family matriarch turned ninety. The guest list for cocktails numbered over five hundred people—family, extended family, friends, and important business clients of the family. Aunt Roberta had outdone herself in organizing the evening. In another hour and a half, there would be a somewhat more intimate dinner, with only about two hundred guests, most of whom were family. Her grandmother was certainly in her element, Edwina thought. But if she had the choice, Edwina would have been anywhere else besides this event. Crowds like this were definitely not her preferred place to be. She needed to get out of this room.

Klaus had given her so much to think about earlier in the day. She hadn't been able to shake the thoughts from her mind. Klaus was a vampire. Father Sabastien was a vampire. Dr. Roddenberg was a vampire. She wondered how many other people she had known over the years were afflicted with this set of acquired abnormalities or something similar.

She stood at the verandah railing for a long time, looking at the lights reflect off the lake near the clubhouse.

Grandmother hadn't been pleased to see Edwina alone tonight.

She had to face the fact that she had fallen irrevocably in love with Klaus. The dreams just reinforced that need that she felt for him. She sighed. What she didn't know was what she was going to do about it. Could she live her life in his state of life? If she didn't transition, could she live out her life knowing that she was only an episode in his life when he was everything to her? Could their love survive a hundred years, or more? Loving him for all eternity? Was it possible? People didn't seem to be able to stay together even ten years anymore, let alone the length of time that she would be married to Klaus if she transitioned. And if she didn't stay married to him, could she remain celibately faithful to her marriage vows? It seemed to her that it was difficult enough to live a Christian life when one had only eighty or so years. She couldn't imagine how difficult it would be to live as a practicing Catholic with a virtual eternity of mortal existence stretching before her.

A male hand lightly came to rest on her shoulder. "Edwina?" an all too familiar voice asked.

"Speak of the Devil. Good evening," Edwina replied without turning to look at him.

"The Devil? Is that how you think of me, now, Edwina?" he asked carefully.

"It's an expression, Klaus. 'Speak of the Devil and he's sure to appear.' It means that if you go looking for trouble, you will find it."

"So now I'm trouble. I do not like this, Edwina," he said teasingly. "It grows worse for me by the moment."

She shook her head negatively. "I seem to be wrong all the way around tonight. Maybe I had just better keep quiet."

"You've been out here for a long time," he said. "Are you cold?"

"No. To tell you the truth, the cold seldom bothers me."

"Do you want to be alone?" he asked.

"I've been alone all my life Klaus," she warned softly. "I don't know how to be anything else. There are times that I wish that I did. I really wish that I did. But I don't. I simply don't know how to be what you need me to be Klaus. And that scares me because I really want to be the kind of wife you need me to be. I just don't know that I can do it."

His hand fell from her shoulder. He came to stand beside her. "All I need you to be is yourself. You know quite well how to do that. Now, come along. You're missing your grandmother's party."

"I'm not needed or even missed in there," she dismissed, still looking at the lake.

"I missed you."

"I didn't even see you in there."

"Probably because I saw you walk out as I walked in," he allowed. "A man could have thought you were avoiding him."

She shrugged. "I just don't like large crowds very much. I didn't know you were on the guest list."

He was silent for a long moment. "Do you think I would crash a party?"

"I think that you would do anything you believed necessary in order to get what you want," she said thoughtfully, still not looking at him. "And you've decided that you want me."

He laughed in genuine amusement.

Oh, how she loved hearing that sound. It frightened her how much she loved hearing him laugh.

"Oh, Edwina, you know me too well. I will indeed do anything I have to do to get what I want. And I do want you, far more than I have ever wanted anyone in my entire life," he agreed. "But if it sets your mind at ease I was invited to this gathering. Richard invited me yesterday. If it sets your mind at ease, I do know your uncle through the local Medical Association. We have met several times over the years. In fact, there are a number of people inside who can vouch for me. Shall I parade them past you? Perhaps twenty or thirty character references will let you feel safe."

"I don't believe that anything would make me feel safe today. I'm trying to work this out in my mind, Klaus. I really am."

"Edwina," he asked in concern. "What specifically troubles you?"

Edwina sighed heavily. "You have given me much to think about Klaus."

"Do you believe that I would ever allow harm to come to you, by my hand or by any other?"

"No."

"You haven't even looked at me tonight Edwina," he said quietly.

"I'm too fragile, too vulnerable, at the moment, Klaus. And it would be too tempting to rely on your invulnerable strength right now."

He put his arm around her shoulder. "'Fragile' is one attribution I would never make about you."

"But then you don't know me that well do you?" she asked in a tight voice.

"Do you think that I would ever harm you?" Klaus asked quietly.

"I don't want to think that, Klaus. I don't really know you. Marriage involves total trust, Klaus. And I'm not sure that I can trust you that much."

"You know me better than most people do."

"That's not saying much Klaus. I don't think you let too many people get close to you."

"I have family and a circle of close friends Edwina."

"Karen's a nice young woman."

"When she's not being a total brat, yes," Klaus agreed.

"She works for you?"

"She works for the corporation."

"She said that she's read my work."

"That's her job—to keep up on new developments. If there is a development on the cutting edge, it's her job to know about it and brief the rest of us as to the work being done and what the ramifications of that work is."

"What kind of ramifications?"

"Primarily ethical. Her master's degree is in biology. Her doctorate is in biomedical ethics."

"What do your other sisters do?"

"Marta is at home with her six children and writes fiction that she has yet to find a market for. Her college degrees are in French Literature. Her husband is a trauma surgeon. They live in the south of France. Sieglinde teaches History at the University of Bonn. Her husband teaches Chemistry there."

"Speaking of family and close friends," Edwina said on a sigh as she removed her dream journal from her purse. "Do you know any of these faces?" she said as she opened the book to the pages in which she had drawn the party from her dream.

Klaus took the book from her fingers. He looked at it. "Where did you get this?"

"Drew it from the dream I had last night. I recognize only Karen and you. Do you know any of other these people?"

"They're my sisters and their husbands. But I don't know this last man here."

"Neither do I," Edwina said. "But he's the one Karen will marry. They seemed awfully familiar with one another in the dream."

"Why did you have this on you if you weren't expecting me?"

"The faces were bothering me. I couldn't get them out of my head. So I put them down on paper. I'd documented most of the dream in my journal early this morning while you were dressing but the faces were still bothering me. Dreams don't give me peace until I fully document them. I hadn't had time today. Earlier this morning, the faces were eluding me. They came to me gradually during the day. So I brought the book and hid out in the ladies room drawing them."

"What kind of dream was it?"

"It was a Christmas party at your house."

Klaus was silent for a long moment. "Any idea of when this dream was set?"

It was Edwina's turn to be silent.

"Edwina?"

She sighed. "Someone, this man," Edwina said pointing at a face, "Said something about your still being able to make me blush after over two years of marriage and a baby."

"How much more confirmation do you need about how right we are together?" Klaus demanded softly.

"I don't know, Klaus. I'm frightened."

"I understand how you would be frightened."

She sighed.

"Marry me, Edwina."

"That would make my grandmother happy."

"Why did you say that?"

"After years and years of chasing away unsuitable potential mates from her grandchildren, Grandmother has finally decided that we're all getting rather long in the tooth and that it's imperative that all of her grandchildren wed soon. So she's put a bounty on the first legitimate great grandchild in order to encourage us to produce that next generation."

"A bounty?"

"Five million dollars will be set up in trust for the first legitimate great grandchild who is baptized into the Catholic faith. The money will be placed into the account on the day of the christening."

"That's a large sum of money."

"It's bribery. None of us will have anything to do with it."

Klaus touched her face lightly. "So, I'm caught here with my suit. You won't say 'yes' because you don't want to give into pressure from your family to wed. Even though you aren't giving into their pressure you don't want it to appear that way."

Edwina sighed. "You make it sound ridiculous."

"Isn't it? What does the money matter if you are following your heart?"

"I've been called 'heartless'," Edwina warned.

"You could never be cruel."

"You sound very sure of that."

"I am."

Edwina sighed again.

"As for the money, it doesn't matter to me at all. Our children will be well provided for whether that sum of money is there or not," Klaus dismissed.

"Assuming there are children."

"If there aren't children, I am certain it won't be for any lack of trying," he said quietly. "I can think of little I would like more than to see you carrying our child."

Edwina felt her face grow warm as she remembered how he had loved her less than twelve hours ago. Had it been only that short of a time ago? It seemed an eternity since they had lain together. "No. I doubt that lack of opportunity would be a problem," she said dryly. "We're going to be amazingly fertile together, you and I."

"You sound sure of that. Another dream?"

"It wasn't one dream. It was a collection of them filling my sleeping hours over several years."

"*Liebling,*" he said gently urging her into his arms. "If you don't want to go back into the party then come with me. Spend some time with me tonight."

"I can't Klaus. I have an obligation to my grandmother. I can't just cut out of her birthday party."

"Is that the only reason you won't come away from here with me?"

She sighed. "Kiss me?"

He didn't have to be asked twice. The caress started light. But like the kisses that had come before, it didn't stay sweet for long.

Fire. That was the only word for him, she thought. He was fire and she was very dry kindling.

Klaus broke the caress and drew her more tightly into his arms. "Neither of us are children, Edwina," he said in German.

"Why do you want to marry me?"

"That, my pet," he said in rapid German, "Should be obvious."

"Sex?"

"That's part of it, but only part. I find that I need you, Edwina, as I've never needed anyone else. You are as essential to me as breathing. I know that you don't feel the same way."

"What makes you think I don't?"

Klaus loosened his embrace on her and stepped back. "Have I become essential to you?"

"I believe you may have become as essential to me as the air I breathe. And that frightens me tremendously."

"I am not a patient man," he told her. "But I've told you that before."

"Klaus, I just haven't yet figured out what you want from me. And to what lengths you are willing to go to get it."

"Haven't you? I thought I was clear on that. I want you. And I will go to any lengths I have to go in order to get you."

She sighed. "I've been warned about you."

"Warned?" he asked carefully. "By whom?"

She shook her head from side to side. "You wouldn't believe me if I told you."

"Try me anyway."

"Catherine."

"Your resident ghost. Now why doesn't that surprise me?" Klaus answered dryly.

"She told me from the first that you were not the man for me, that you were dangerous."

"And you believe her?"

"No. I prefer to make my own decisions."

"And have you made a decision?"

"I need to think this out more."

The sounds of the party invaded the verandah. Edwina knew that someone had opened a door.

"Hey, Winnie, what's up? *Granmere* is looking for you," Marie said in concern.

Edwina sighed. "I'll be right there, Marie."

Marie laughed and threw back her head. "I can see Winnie that you will have the money," she said in French.

"If you want it then go for it Marie," Edwina encouraged her cousin. "I'm not interested."

"No. Not me. I'm not going to get married and have a baby just so that I could get five million dollars from *Granmere*, especially as it will be in trust for the child."

"What makes you think I would?" Edwina asked coldly.

Marie shook her head. "It's different with you, Winnie. You're not doing it for the money. A blind man could see the attraction between the two of you. You're out here together in this weather instead of being warm inside. That has to mean something."

"I think it means that I'm growing cold. Excuse me," Edwina said quietly.

Klaus followed her inside. The band was playing dance music from the 1940s. It was upbeat and called out to be danced to. He took her by the hand and led her out onto the dance floor.

"Just what do you think you're doing?" Edwina demanded of Klaus.

"Dancing with you," he said. "If you do not wish to dance then walk away from me."

Edwina smiled. "You know that I can't do that. There are too many people watching us. I wouldn't cause that kind of embarrassment to my worst enemy."

Klaus smiled as he pulled her closer to him. "And I am not your worst enemy."

"Pull another stunt like this and I may move you way up on my list," Edwina warned. "I don't dance well and everyone is looking at us."

He laughed softly. "I'm trembling with fear."

"It amazes me sometimes that you and your ego can both fit in one suit of clothes," she said dryly.

He chuckled again. Then he lightly kissed her forehead. The song died off.

"I need something to drink. Excuse me."

"I will join you."

Edwina walked over to the bar. "Club soda and lime," she ordered.

Klaus asked for a vodka gimlet.

No sooner had they turned around than her Uncle John was right there. "Edwina, your grandmother wishes for you and your gentleman friend to join her at her table for dinner."

Refusing a summons from Grandmother would be unthinkable if one wished to live in peace with her family. Edwina knew this. Grandmother ruled the family with an iron fist inside a velvet glove.

"Of course, Uncle," Edwina replied quietly. "I trust that Aunt Roberta is busily rearranging the seating arrangements as we speak?"

He smiled. "I believe that she has completed that task."

"Then you'll excuse us?"

"Go have fun. Someone needs to. You should be warned, your Grandmother has gathered the senior members of the clan at her table, along with both of you."

Edwina rolled her eyes. "I see."

Uncle James smiled. "For what it's worth, Edwina, I know that you can give back as good as you get." Then he walked away.

She sighed.

"What was that about?" Klaus asked.

She looked at Klaus. "I didn't plan this," she told him quietly in German.

"I take it that this will be tantamount to the Inquisition?"

"They'll probably be nicer than Torquemada," Edwina said lowly. "The torture will be purely verbal."

He squeezed her hand. "I'll handle it."

"I warned you. Grandmother is a Tartar."

"I've managed Tartars before."

"My grandmother is unique."

"Of course she is. You are her granddaughter."

Edwina introduced Klaus to everyone at the table.

"Just how long have you been interested in my granddaughter, *Herr* von Bruner?" Grandmother asked without prelude.

Klaus smiled. "I've been following her work since her genetics dissertation was brought to my attention seven years ago. The work she did there was nothing short of amazing."

Grandmother nodded. "There were people who chose to use different words to describe it. Sometimes in far less complimentary terms."

Klaus nodded. "Then again there are always people who will fear anything truly new and revolutionary or who will fail to see the potential for any far reaching study."

Grandmother smiled at him. "Oh, they saw the potential and it scared them to death," she acknowledged.

"I know that once I thought about it her work frightened me in some of its implications. My granddaughter has the Walker backbone. She is like me, *Herr* von Bruner, in that she is a velvet glove over an iron fist."

"From what I've seen of your family, M'am, most of your relatives share that trait. Whether it is genetic or merely a trait adopted as a matter of self-defense remains to be seen. I do suspect however, that both factors may be active."

Grandmother looked at him for a long moment in the utter silence that had fallen over the table. Then she laughed, boldly. Everyone else laughed, mostly in relief.

Edwina kissed Klaus on the cheek.

"I like you, Klaus von Bruner," Grandmother stated, giving her ultimate seal of approval. "Edwina, when do you plan to marry this man?"

"I have not yet accepted his offer of marriage, Grandmother."

The old woman looked at Edwina with those piercing blue eyes. "Why not?"

"That, my dear, is none of your concern," Edwina told her grandmother gently. "It is something Klaus and I need to work out by ourselves."

"Falderal," the old woman dismissed. "You have never been a fool, my dear. Don't launch a career as a ninny-hammer at this late date. Marriage is always a family affair. It unites two families. I don't see any need for delay. Neither of you is still wet behind the ears. In fact, both of you are of what my generation would consider rather ripe in years for a first marriage."

Then the old woman looked thoughtfully at the pair. "Or are you both enjoying the sex so much that you don't want to spoil the romance with marriage? I understand that this is how things are generally done these days among the younger set."

Edwina was sipping her white wine as her grandmother made that comment. It was all she could do not to splutter. She swallowed and glared at her grandmother. Through gritted teeth, she told the old woman in no uncertain terms, "My love life is none of your business, Grandmother."

Klaus took her hand. "You are definitely her grandchild, Edwina. She is as amazingly perceptive as you are. And both of you have a tongue that slices like a razor," he said quietly in rapid German.

Edwina felt her face grow hot and knew that she was blushing brightly. "My grandmother speaks German as do all the rest of my family," she said quietly in rapid German.

"They are all adults. They know that sexual attraction is a big part of a couple's falling in love. And they have eyes to see how dearly I love you, Edwina," he replied in his native language. "I wish that you would give me the answer I want to hear in connection with my offer of marriage."

"I've told you. I won't be rushed, Klaus. Marriage is too serious of a decision to make in a hurry. We haven't really known each other that long. Marriage is something that we will have to live with for the rest of our lives."

"I can think of nothing I would like better than to spend the rest of my life with you," Klaus said quietly.

"You are entirely impossible!" she replied on a sigh.

Klaus smiled. "Then my dearest, we are a matched pair."

"Things come entirely too easy for you, Klaus."

"Which means that you intend to lead me a merry chase," he said, clearly amused.

"I sincerely doubt that anyone could lead you anywhere that you did not want to go."

"Another way that we are remarkably matched."

"It would appear so, *Herr* Baron," her grandmother answered in German. "But my granddaughter is stubborn."

"Gracious lady," he answered in his native language, "We shall have to see who is the more stubborn. I shall not take 'no' for an answer. I think perhaps, it is a matter that Edwina does not trust her own dreams," Klaus offered.

The table fell silent. Edwina's dreaming was an open secret that no one talked about because it made certain members of the family completely uncomfortable. That this stranger should know of it was astonishing to them.

"Dreams?" her grandmother demanded. "You have been dreaming again, Edwina?"

"'Again' is not the proper term. I've never stopped," Edwina answered in rapid German.

"And how long have you been dreaming of *Herr* Baron von Bruner?" her grandmother demanded.

Edwina was visibly embarrassed. "A very long time, Grandmother."

"A long time? How long?" her grandmother insisted in a strained voice.

Edwina blushed. She didn't want to give this answer. It was more information than she wanted Klaus to have. But she wasn't going to lie or hedge. "Twenty-five years, Grandmother."

Klaus looked at her in surprise. "Twenty-five years? You didn't tell me the dreams were of that duration."

"This is something for us to discuss at a later time, when we can be alone," Edwina said.

Everyone at the table was quiet for a very long time. Then Edwina's grandmother nodded and spoke in a gentle tone, "I see. Then he is hardly a stranger to you, is he?"

"I do believe that he is a stranger to most people. A polite, affable stranger in social situations. A formidable stranger in business situations. But a stranger none-the-less in most situations to most people. There are precious few to whom he grants the privilege of getting past his incredibly well defended walls."

Klaus chuckled. "You know me too well, my dear."

"I know you hardly at all, Klaus," Edwina replied.

"You will."

She looked at him for a long moment before replying, "I can't decide if that is a threat or a promise."

"I never make threats," Klaus replied smoothly. "They are an utter waste of time."

Edwina picked up her glass and drank some of the very expensive wine. "No. You would not make threats. You are more akin to a steamroller than anything else. Heaven help anyone who gets in your way."

Klaus only smiled. "Is it not like looking in a mirror, Edwina Elizabeth?"

Her grandmother demanded, "When is the wedding?"

"Right before Lent," Klaus said quietly. "My cousin, Father Wilhelm, is coming in from his post at the Vatican on the Monday before Ash Wednesday. His boss had a heart to heart with the Nuncio, who talked to the Cardinal. All the paperwork has been taken care of and smoothed away to allow Willie to officiate at the marriage. The pre-Cana instruction is being handled by Fr. Sabastien who is chaplain to my corporation. And Willie is bringing with him a certificate of Papal Blessing on this marriage."

"You are certainly pulling out all the stops, aren't you?" Edwina demanded.

"I'm usually not hesitant to go after what I want. But you know that."

Edwina sighed. "And what would you do if I said I wouldn't marry you?"

Klaus smiled. "We have your parish for the evening of Mardi Gras. The florist has already been contacted and the flowers ordered. The reception will be at my house. Your uncle Richard will certify the blood work for the marriage license."

Edwina shook her head with a sigh. "You still haven't answered my question. What would you do if I said I wouldn't marry you?"

"Are you saying that, Edwina?"

"No. I think I would rather cut out my tongue with a butter knife than to say that." Edwina was shocked at herself for her bluntness.

Klaus smiled. "I see I'm rubbing off on you. You are becoming more willing to speak your mind."

She couldn't help it. She laughed. "You are impossible, Klaus Matthias."

"So I've been told many times."

"I suppose that you've already called your sisters and they'll be here?"

"Of course."

"Well, then I guess that I had better take that engagement ring."

"The wedding is less than two weeks away," her grandmother stated as Klaus produced the ring box from his pocket and slid the emerald onto her finger. "How in the world do you expect her family to be ready in that short of a time?"

"The only thing you have to do is to be there. Everything else is taken care of," Klaus told her grandmother.

"It is the bride's family's responsibility to see to the details of the wedding and reception," her grandmother said firmly. "How in the world is she to have time to acquire a bridal gown, let alone bridesmaids dresses? Florists and caterers are not easy to come by at short notice."

"I have my mother's bridal gown in storage in your attic, Grandmother. As for bridesmaids dresses, flowers, caterers, etc. I really don't care one way or another. All we need is one witness each to sign the register and the license. Ockham's Razor applies."

"Ockham's Razor?" her aunt Roberta asked.

Edwina sipped her wine while Klaus explained the reference. "One statement of that principle is 'It is vain to do with more, what can be done with less.' William of Ockham was a Franciscan in the fourteenth century, if memory serves, taught at Cambridge."

Uncle Lawrence smiled broadly. "Well, Edwina, looks like you have found a man who can keep up with you."

Edwina chuckled. "I have to run to keep up with *him*."

"That should be a change for you," Uncle Lawrence replied with a smile.

Her grandmother smiled and stood. She motioned for silence. When the room was quiet, she said, "Thank you all for coming to my birthday party. This has been simply a lovely evening. Yet, it has been made lovelier by a gift of joy. My granddaughter Edwina has just announced her impending marriage to Klaus von Bruner. Stand and join me in drinking to the health and happiness of Edwina and Klaus... Edwina, Klaus, may God bless both of you with patience, courage, and peace to accompany the love we already see in your eyes."

Everyone raised their glasses. Edwina felt her face grow warm.

Klaus squeezed her hand after the toast was completed. "I am glad that you are being so sensible about this."

"I usually am sensible," Edwina replied sharply.

He smiled at her. "I am aware of this."

Edwina's cell phone rang.

"You know how I feel about those instruments," her grandmother said quietly in a quite displeased tone.

"Excuse me, Grandmother," Edwina said as she rose to her feet and walked away from the table in order to take the call.

"Ed," a frantic female voice said over the phone.

"Jennifer?"

"You aren't in the shop are you?"

"No. I'm at Grandmother's birthday party. Why?"

"I just turned on the news. The building is in flames. It's terrible. The fire department is saying that the blaze is out totally of control."

"Thank you for calling, Jennifer. This will not affect anything with the nursery."

"I'm just glad you weren't in the building."

"Brenda was in charge of closing up tonight. It's not yet closing time. She may have been in the building," Edwina said quietly.

"I'll check."

"Call me back. I'll call my insurance agent."

She removed her personal directory from her evening bag and dialed the number for the home of the insurance agent.

"Luke, Edwina Johnson. I've just heard a report that my building is ablaze."

"I'll verify that and get back with you. You're calling on the cell?"

"Yes. Thanks."

Edwina returned to her seat. She placed the cell phone on the table.

"What was so important?" Grandmother asked.

"My building is on fire, apparently out of control," Edwina said in a deceptively calm voice. But no one at the table missed how her hand was shaking as she tried to take a sip of her wine.

The phone rang again. "Johnson," she answered the phone on the first ring.

"Brenda's unaccounted for," Jennifer said quietly.

"God's mercy. We can only hope that she got out," Edwina said, her voice strained. "Thank you for calling."

"Edwina," Klaus said gently. "What is it?"

"My clerk is unaccounted for. She may be inside the building yet. I have to go there. Grandmother, I am sorry that this intruded on your celebration. But I need to be there. I have to know."

"Pah, child, life is full of events that none of us can plan. You will take up residence with me as your apartment will be uninhabitable or destroyed in this fire." Her grandmother handed her a key to her house. "Go and be safe."

"Thank you, Grandmother," Edwina said quietly. "I appreciate the shelter."

"We will replace your wardrobe tomorrow, child."

Edwina sighed. "I must go."

Her grandmother nodded. "Of course, you must. Klaus, you will take care of her?"

"Of course, madam."

Klaus rose from the table. "I will see you safely to your Grandmother's, after you survey the damage."

Uncle Lawrence rose as well. "You'll need your lawyer, especially in light of the threat from your tenant."

"Threat?" Grandmother demanded.

Edwina sighed. "I have to go. I'll explain later."

"Indeed you shall, Edwina," Grandmother replied firmly. "Indeed you shall."

Chapter Eleven

The area was cordoned off seven blocks in each direction of the fire. Even from that distance the fire looked terrible. Clouds of black smoke and bright flames danced together. It seemed as though every fire truck in the metropolitan area was out, but they weren't fighting the fire in her building. They were merely trying to keep the flames from spreading.

Edwina didn't want to think about the damage to the buildings surrounding this. She had incorporated the shop on the advice of Uncle Lawrence. The assets of each of the segments of her estate were minimal. She had incorporated the holding company in which the title to the building was held. The assets there were also minimal. Everything she owned was well insured and her uncle had done his best to protect her by isolating the various items of her holdings so that they would be untouchable by lien or lawsuit against any other part of her personal holdings.

She supposed that property owners on every side — or their insurance companies — could always petition the courts to do what lawyers called "piercing the veil of the corporation", or holding her personally responsible for the damage to their property, or worse yet, for the loss of life she feared was likely. Yet there was the police report about the threat from Jim to burn down the building. She had done all she could reasonably be expected to do to prevent this from happening. Hadn't she?

As she stood watching the horror of it all, Klaus held her tightly at his side.

A television reporter from one of the local stations came over to her along with the cameraman. The lights shone in her face. "They tell me that you own the building that is burning?"

Edwina focused in on the reporter's face. She sighed raggedly as she fought hard for her self-control. Dealing with watching her dreams literally go up in smoke was the hardest thing that she had ever done. Knowing that people might be dead in the process was breaking her heart. All she wanted to do was cry, curl up in a little ball, and let someone else take care of everything for a little while. But she couldn't do that. To make a public display of her emotions ran counter to all of her training. That kind of indoctrination in self-control ran deep. "Yes. It's my building," she said, her voice breaking under the strain.

"What do you suppose caused the fire?" the reporter asked.

Edwina shook her head negatively. "I don't know. At the moment, I really don't care," Edwina dismissed as tears welled up in her eyes. She blinked them back, then bit her quivering bottom lip. "My only real concern is for the people in the building. Things are only things. They can be replaced. But lives are unique. A part-time employee, Brenda Carstairs, was in my shop. Brenda, if you got out, call me on my cell phone. Any of my tenants who got out, call me, please."

"No one has been able to get close enough to the building after the initial explosion to get anyone out," the reporter said compassionately. "I'm sorry."

Edwina fought, and lost, the battle with tears. She crossed herself. "It's a terrible thing!" She dashed the tears from her cheeks and forced herself to regain some measure of composure. "There were several shops in the building that stayed open late. There could have easily been people in all of them."

"But you weren't there tonight obviously."

"No. I was at a family celebration."

"There was a fire in this building on Saturday night," the reporter countered.

"Early Sunday morning. It was a small fire in one of the street level shops and was easily controlled. The sprinkler system was inspected and repaired Sunday afternoon. It was in working order today."

"My police sources tell me there was a threat made against the building."

"Yes. One of my tenants—the same one who had the fire on Sunday morning—has repeatedly asserted he believes his shop to be haunted. He left remarks on my answering machine that he intended to burn down the building in order to exorcise the poltergeists he claimed were wrecking his business."

"You think he's behind this?" the reporter asked.

"I don't know," Edwina said raggedly, tears beginning to fall once more. She removed her eyeglasses with her left hand and scrubbed the tears from her face with her right. Then she replaced her eyeglasses. "I have my suspicions. But I just don't know. The only thing that I'm sure of is that my tenant needs a lot of help holding onto reality. I was trying to get him help. I'd sworn out a complaint charging that his mental condition made him a threat to himself and others and asking that he be placed under psychiatric observation. I didn't know what else to do. He'd gotten violent with me. He'd been issuing threats." She sighed raggedly. "I even warned the tenants to watch out for him, and told them what was going on, after I'd filed the report with the police about the threats."

"The fire department says the reason they can't get the fire out is that there is a lot of fuel in the building."

Edwina sighed. "I suppose that's right. The street level shops all had lots of chemicals in them. There was a paint and wallpaper store, a dry cleaners, a garden shop, and an art supply store. "

"That's quite a collection of shops."

She sighed again. "Except for the garden shop, they were all here when I bought the building." She looked at the building and felt herself tear up again. "I'm sorry. I don't think I can answer any more questions without becoming a blubbering idiot. This is very hard."

"Come on, *Liebling*," Klaus said in rapid German with tenderness in his voice. He turned her away from the barricade and urged her to walk away with him. "There is nothing more that you can do here. Tomorrow will be a long day. You need to rest."

"How can I rest?" she answered him in equally rapid German.

"I will see that you sleep," Klaus answered, retaining the German. "I can give you an injection to aid you to sleep."

"No. I don't think so, Klaus," she replied in German as she kept pace with him. "I will not depend on drugs for sleep. Not even after a horror like this."

"There is nothing to be done here."

"No. There is nothing further I can do here, tonight. I wonder if Heather and Phlox got out."

"Cats are resilient creatures, Edwina. If they don't turn up, I'll get you two new cats. You can name them Tulip and Rose."

Edwina sighed and shook her head. When she spoke, there was heat in her voice, "I'm not ready for other cats. I love those cats. Pets are not like panes of glass! When one breaks, you don't just replace it with something identical."

"Calm down," Klaus said.

"I don't want to calm down, my business, my apartment, almost everything that I own were in that building. Several people that I care about may be in that building. I don't want to be calm. I want to scream, throw a temper tantrum, and break things."

Klaus looked at her. "I understand. But I'm not your enemy."

She sighed raggedly. "No. You are my love."

Klaus kissed her forehead. "Whatever comes, we'll get through this together, Edwina."

"Heather and Phlox just showed up on my doorstep one morning after my parents died. I tried very hard to find their owners. No one ever claimed them. The vet said that they were in good health, aside from being a little on the thin side. So I kept them and they kept me company. They were smart cats. I had a kitty door for them through the greenhouse out onto the fire escape. They might have gotten out."

"They probably are fine," Klaus allowed.

"I can't stand the thought of their burning to death, Klaus. I can't stand it."

"I know."

Klaus handed her into his car. "I'm more of a dog person. But I understand what you are saying."

Edwina curled up against Klaus and put her head on his shoulder as they drove towards her grandmother's house. The privacy panel still separated them from the driver.

She began to sob.

Klaus hated to hear that sound. She was crying as though her heart was breaking. He felt helpless.

"It's always hard to lose a home," Klaus said quietly when she had just about brought herself back under control.

"I really tried to make a home for myself there."

"You did a wonderful job of it."

"Were you comfortable there?"

"Yes."

"All my father's books are gone," she said lowly. "My photographs. Mother's violin. Nothing can ever replace those things."

Her cell phone rang. She answered it, "Johnson."

"Ed, it's Jen. Brenda's okay. She just called me."

"Thank God!"

"The front of the building exploded, and she ran out the back and kept running."

"Smart woman! Thanks for letting me know."

"Hang tight, Ed. If there is anything you need, let me know."

"Thanks, Jen. I appreciate it."

Klaus smiled at her. "You look like you just had a big weight removed from your shoulders."

"My employee is safe. Brenda got out."

"I'm sure the cats did too."

There was something in his tone, but she couldn't decipher it.

She saw the signs for a strip mall ahead. She just realized that she had nothing. "Klaus, I need to stop and buy some things. Do you mind?"

"Not at all."

The anchor store of the strip mall was a national discount store that stayed open twenty-four hours. Klaus accompanied her inside as Edwina quickly picked out essentials. Her cart contained only what she would absolutely need for the next few days, yet it was still quite full by the time that she was ready to pay for her items.

"You shop quickly," he observed.

"I hate shopping. Anything that is necessary that I hate this much, I do quickly."

Klaus kissed her temple. "Are you done?"

"Yes. Let's get out of here."

When they were back in the car, he asked, "Edwina, do you want me to set you aside some lab space?" Perhaps the change in subjects would help keep her mind off of the fire.

"I would like some greenhouse space and a small lab, yes."

"Are you thinking of anything related to the work on improving UV tolerance?"

"Yes. But I think I need to do some intense reading before I begin that work. I'm a botanist at heart, Klaus. I'm not really up to speed on anything related to human genetics. I'm definitely not up to speed on anything to do with these abnormalities. I'll want DNA markers from a representative sampling of the population."

"Would two hundred subjects do?"

"I don't know. It ought to be a start at least. How big is the population?"

"There are fifty thousand of us, at the last census."

"When was the last census?"

"The results came out two months ago. The count was made six months ago."

"And how many refused to be officially counted?"

"That's the issue. There are many people who remember only too well angry mobs of vampire hunters. Those individuals will not register out of fear the registry could fall into the wrong hands. Best guess is that there are another ten to eleven thousand. There are about a thousand people whom no one has reported seeing for at least a decade. Whether they are still alive or have died is an open question."

"I see. Case studies would help to go along with the markers."

"They're all in the files, waiting for you to be ready for them."

"This scares me, Klaus."

"I understand that. If it helps at all, I think you are doing famously with this situation."

"Are any of the women from your group with whom you have had children still alive?" Edwina asked uncertainly.

"No. And before you ask the following logical question, you aren't one of my descendants."

"That about covers all the bases."

"Not quite," Klaus said.

"What else do we need to cover?"

"Will you join me in my state of life? Or will you remain a normal human?"

"I don't know, Klaus. I need time to think. It's a big decision. And it's not one on which I can seek counsel. No one among the normal population would believe me. And those of your kind have an agenda."

He sighed. "Very well, Edwina. When you have made a decision, let me know. Just don't wait too long. The transition stops aging, but nothing reverses the process. Transitioning allows one to heal rapidly from most injuries, but it doesn't repair old injuries. Transitioning a pregnant woman is also transitioning her unborn child which, as it stops growth and development, is not advisable."

"Even more for me to think about."

"Could you be pregnant now?"

"Unlikely. My cycle is due in a couple of days."

"Which means that you might become pregnant on our wedding night?"

"I doubt it. It doesn't fit the dreams. We'll have a little time until parenthood."

"You are beginning to believe your dreams?"

"I've always fought believing in them. I haven't wanted to surrender that much control over my life."

"Control is important to you."

"I've come to the conclusion that the only thing I can control is myself. And I can't always do that."

Schmidt drove them the rest of the way to her grandmother's house. The silence between them was companionable for the rest of the drive. Edwina sat next to Klaus, her head on his shoulder, his arm about her holding her gently.

"Will you come in?"

Klaus nodded. Schmidt helped her out of the car, and instructed the driver to wait. When Edwina climbed up onto the porch of her grandmother's house, she was met by the sound of mewing. There were Heather and Phlox, waiting for her.

"How in the world...?" Edwina exclaimed as she dropped the bags and caught the cats as they jumped into her arms. She looked at Klaus and saw that he looked guilty.

"Okay, what's going on?" she demanded as the cats jumped out of her arms and back onto the porch decking.

"Edwina," Klaus began hesitantly. "You know that I love you."

"Why do I think I don't want to hear the rest of this?"

"Because you don't. Show her Heather, and you too, Phlox."

Edwina looked at the cats that suddenly morphed into a man and a woman. They were dressed simply in dancer's leotards and tights of the same color as the cats' fur.

"Lycanthropes." She turned to Klaus. "How long have you known?"

"A long time," Klaus admitted. "I sent Penny and Jack, whom you knew as Heather and Phlox, to you as personal protectors. It was their job to keep you safe. If there had been any physical danger, they would have changed form and dealt with it."

Edwina looked at him and sighed.

"Don't be angry, Edwina," Penny, Heather cat, said quietly.

She sighed again. "I'm not angry."

"Aren't you?" Jack demanded.

"Oddly enough, I'm relieved that you got out. If you had been just normal cats, you might not have gotten out of the fire," Edwina told them. "I've grown fond of you two."

Penny smiled. "And we've enjoyed the assignment. It isn't often that we can serve such a kind woman. Jack and I wish you every happiness. *Herr* Baron, you will get our bill."

"Stay on patrol," Klaus told them. "We're not certain this is over. The arsonist may have gotten out of the building. She may still be in danger."

"Of course," Jack answered just before he morphed back into the Seal Point Siamese.

Edwina shook her head negatively and sighed. "I see I am simply going to have to start believing three impossible things each morning before breakfast."

Klaus chuckled. "You're taking this well."

"You would prefer that I indulge in hysterics?"

"No, you aren't the type for hysterics. You've been trained all your life to be steady, grounded, and calmly controlled. That training has helped you become the woman you are and will be the basis for the woman you will become. "

"Since I met you, I don't feel either calm or controlled."

"Good. I want every bit of the passion of your soul."

She sighed. "You may not like what you find there."

Klaus dropped a kiss on her forehead. "I love you. Everything else is secondary. Come on. Let's get you settled in."

Louella met them at the door. "Come in, honey," the housekeeper said. "And you've brought your young man with you. She is going to like that."

"Which room does Grandmother want me in?"

"Top of the stairs on your left, same room you had when you came as a child to visit her."

"I'm going to put these things away, then Klaus and I are going into the attic to look for some things."

"Okay, honey. If you need help, just holler."

"Right, Louella. Thanks."

Klaus stood at the door to her childhood room as she put away the few new items she had bought. The cats settled in readily on the window seat. It was obvious that the furnishings hadn't been changed much over the years. The bed was definitely too short for her.

"Are you going to be comfortable here?" he asked carefully.

"It's just a place to sleep, Klaus, until the wedding."

"You could have a room at my house. Karen's there to chaperone."

"No. I'll stay with my grandmother until the wedding. Then I'll move in with you and not before. Come on, we've got looking to do in the attic."

"For what?"

"I've stored some of my parents' things up here. My mother's wedding gown. Her silver. Her china. Some of their furniture I couldn't bear to get rid of. And some other things."

They climbed up into the attic. The cats followed her.

After about an hour of looking, they had found most of the things that Edwina wanted. The temperature in the attic lowered by ten degrees.

The cats began to yowl.

"She's here," Edwina said quietly to Klaus.

"What do you want, Spirit?" Klaus addressed the entity.

Catherine's form materialized before them. "Edwina, you don't know what this creature is."

"I know," Edwina said firmly.

"Do you? Look in the second box to your left. It has the old photo we spoke of. Look at it, now."

"I don't need to," Edwina said firmly. "And you can go away and never bother me again. You are not welcome in my grandmother's house."

"He's controlling you. Can't you see that?" Catherine demanded.

"No one is controlling me," Edwina denied flatly.

"You poor fool," the spirit said as she faded out. "You poor deluded fool. He's going to destroy you."

"What photo did she want you to see?"

"Johann and Regina."

Klaus nodded. "She was very much like you in appearance. Regina was shorter than you are. She was somewhat plumper. She was a kind and gentle soul who never had a bad comment to make about anyone."

"You knew her well?"

"She was my son's wife, not mine, Edwina, if that is what you are asking. And she was a lovely woman who died at a far too young age, as many women once died, in childbirth."

"Her child lived?"

"For about another year or so. I took his place when he died after a bout with scarlet fever."

"I see."

"What are you thinking?"

She took his hand. "We had better get some of this stuff downstairs. I'll need to check Mother's wedding gown to see if it's intact."

"And if it isn't?"

"It's not that important, Klaus. It's just a dress. I can get another dress."

"What is important, Edwina?"

"Loving you. Helping you by engineering a retrovirus that will eliminate the side effects from this condition. Those are the important things."

"You know that work could take decades, maybe a century or more."

She sighed. "Yes, it might. I've got a leg up on it. I have my research notes that led to the development of the retrovirus."

He looked at her carefully. "You have future research notes from a successful retrovirus? How do you have this?"

"From my dreams."

"You recorded research in your dreams?"

"Come on down to Grandmother's office. I'll show you the notes when I download them from the remote backup computer. I've always kept a backup of all my work on an off-site system. Grab the box with Mother's wedding gown in it."

They sat in her grandmother's office. Edwina printed off the pages about the research question dream.

Klaus looked them over for close to an hour before he looked up at her.

"Brilliant, Edwina. Absolutely brilliant."

"I will make this work, Klaus."

"Will you transition?"

"I will need to in order to have the time to work on this fully."

"I want you with me, Edwina. I want to share the rest of my life with you."

"I wouldn't be marrying you if I was less than committed to you, Klaus."

He smiled. "Of course, *Liebling*. Can I see more of these diaries of yours?"

"Not tonight Klaus. I can go to the bank tomorrow and get the actual journals out of the lockbox."

"You trust me that much, Edwina, to share your dreams?"

"I trust you with my life, the lives of our future children, and with all I am, have, or will ever have, Klaus. I wouldn't be marrying you otherwise. What are a few thousand dreams in comparison to a life together?"

Epilogue

Klaus and Edwina lay on the beach in the morning sunlight, looking out onto the crystal blue water of the Caribbean. The sound of children laughing filled the air.

"Momma, Papa," a red haired lad of six called out as he ran to them.

"Sean, what is it, sweetheart?" Edwina asked.

"Mary won't let me go in the ocean."

Edwina looked at her dear husband, then at Sean, their youngest child. He was so like all of the fifteen other boys to whom they had given life over the nearly one hundred and seventy years of their marriage. Each of their sons, like their five daughters, had possessed unique and precious personalities. Looking at this child almost brought tears to her eyes. He was so like his father in personality. Of course, Klaus thought that young Sean was so much like her in looks. She frequently teased Klaus that the poor child had the worst of both sets of genes.

He would be small for such a very short time. The child longed to have his childhood behind him and to be all grown-up. Personally, she thought it such a shame that youth was wasted on the young who didn't appreciate it.

"Sean," Klaus reminded the child, "you don't swim well enough to go into the water without someone with you. I told you that we would all go swimming in the protected bay later this afternoon."

Sean's lip pouted out in displeasure.

"Stick that lip out more, and I'll hang a bucket from it," Edwina advised quietly as she pulled the child into her lap and gave him a cuddle before sending him off to play with his brothers and sister.

Engineering a retrovirus had taken much longer than they had either one anticipated, even with her research notes from the dreams. Spending the day outside— lounging on the beach, going to a child's ball game, puttering again in her garden, or just going about doing business like a normal person—had been well worth the prolonged effort.

They had changed identities twice. Klaus had "passed on" first, thirty-three years into their marriage, leaving her a "widow" when their oldest grandson had died suddenly from an a complication of chickenpox. Then, five years later, Edwina had taken on the identity of an unrelated two-year old child, Elizabeth Smith, who had suffered from xeroderma pigmentosum—a rare genetic disease that gave the child an absolute intolerance to sunlight. As a cover story, it hadn't been bad. Young Elizabeth had been twelve when she had challenged the biology department of Yale University for her bachelor's degree in biology. Two years later, she had defended her doctoral dissertation and had been awarded a double Ph.D. in botany and genetics. She had joined a nineteen year old Klaus in the lab. When she had turned seventeen and Klaus was twenty-two, according to the world's reckoning, she had married Klaus all over again. They had lived together until their ninetieth wedding anniversary. Then their elderly forms had been found together in bed, apparently dying entwined in each other's arms as they had slept peacefully. By then, they had created other identities for them to step into, young adult identities of Matthais Klaus von Bruner and Brigid Edwina Carstairs, who soon became a von Bruner.

One time of being separated from one another for all of a childhood, and having been forced to sneak around to see one another in alternate forms, had been all either of them had been willing to endure. The engineering the identities had not been something done quickly but it had been worth the effort. She counted every day with Klaus as a day well spent.

The world still wasn't ready to admit the existence of their kind. So changing identities had been essential. Perhaps one day, it wouldn't be necessary to hide behind names that weren't theirs, just as it was now no longer essential for their kind to hide away from the sun.

For now, however, both she and Klaus were content to live their lives fully, moment by moment, enjoying the pleasure of one another and the joys of life that were theirs. Edwina had been wise enough to take the chance presented by her dream lover.

The End

About the author:

I'm best described as "the Mom next door". Amy Turpin at Timeless Tales, said of my vampire story, Dream Lover, "Forget everything you think you know about vampires. This story creates a refreshing new legend to capture the reader's imagination and makes you look twice at those people insisting upon working the night shift! Ms. Walder tells a wonderful tale that is at once intelligent and engaging." That's always my goal; to write intelligent, engaging, wonderful tales that delight my readers. I love to hear from my readers and they can always contact me at cassie @cassiewalder.com or at cassiewalderproductions @ yahoo.com.

Cassie Walder welcomes mail from readers. You can write to them c/o Ellora's Cave Publishing at P.O. Box 787, Hudson, Ohio 44236-0787.

Also by Cassie Walder:

- Dream Job

Why an electronic book?

We live in the Information Age—an exciting time in the history of human civilization in which technology rules supreme and continues to progress in leaps and bounds every minute of every hour of every day. For a multitude of reasons, more and more avid literary fans are opting to purchase e-books instead of paperbacks. The question to those not yet initiated to the world of electronic reading is simply: *why?*

1. *Price.* An electronic title at Ellora's Cave Publishing runs anywhere from 40-75% less than the cover price of the <u>exact same title</u> in paperback format. Why? Cold mathematics. It is less expensive to publish an e-book than it is to publish a paperback, so the savings are passed along to the consumer.

2. *Space.* Running out of room to house your paperback books? That is one worry you will never have with electronic novels. For a low one-time cost, you can purchase a handheld computer designed specifically for e-reading purposes. Many e-readers are larger than the average handheld, giving you plenty of screen room. Better yet, hundreds of titles can be stored within your new library—a single microchip. (Please note that Ellora's Cave does not endorse any specific brands. You can check our website at *www.ellorascave.com* for customer recommendations we make available to new consumers.)

3. *Mobility.* Because your new library now consists of only a microchip, your entire cache of books can be taken with you wherever you go.

4. *Personal preferences are accounted for.* Are the words you are currently reading too small? Too large? Too...**ANNOYING**? Paperback books cannot be modified according to personal preferences, but e-books can.

5. *Innovation.* The *way* you read a book is not the only advancement the Information Age has gifted the literary community with. There is also the factor of *what* you can read. Ellora's Cave Publishing will be introducing a new line of interactive titles that are available in e-book format only.

6. *Instant gratification.* Is it the middle of the night and all the bookstores are closed? Are you tired of waiting days—sometimes weeks—for online and offline bookstores to ship the novels you bought? Ellora's Cave Publishing sells instantaneous downloads 24 hours a day, 7 days a week, 365 days a year. Our e-book delivery system is 100% automated, meaning your order is filled as soon as you pay for it.

Those are a few of the top reasons why electronic novels are displacing paperbacks for many an avid reader. As always, Ellora's Cave Publishing welcomes your questions and comments. We invite you to email us at service@ellorascave.com or write to us directly at: P.O. Box 787, Hudson, Ohio 44236-0787.

Printed in the United States
23267LVS00003BA/133-210